Breakfast
Served
Anytime

Breakfast Served Anytime

SARAH COMBS

CANDLEWICK PRESS

Copyright © 2014 by Sarah Combs
Butterfly images copyright © 2014 by Francesco Carta
fotografo/Getty Images
Excerpt from *Charlotte's Web* by E. B. White copyright 1952 by
E. B. White, used by permission of the E. B. White Estate.

First edition 2014

Library of Congress Catalog Card Number 2013944002
ISBN 978-0-7636-6791-7

14 15 16 17 18 19 BVG 10 9 8 7 6 5 4 3 2 1

Printed in Berryville, VA, U.S.A.

This book was typeset in Sabon.

Candlewick Press
99 Dover Street
Somerville, Massachusetts 02144

visit us at www.candlewick.com

For the original Geek Campers, especially
Ericka Quezada-York (whose title I stole)
&
Huston Barrow Combs (who stole my heart)

Always be on the watch for the coming of wonders.

—E. B. WHITE

1

Into the Abyss

THE BUTTERFLIES started showing up the night before I left for Geek Camp. The first one came as a surprise: an otherworldly blue messenger, lifting and settling its wings on the windshield of the wheezy Chrysler LeBaron I had inherited from my grandmother just months before. Carol was riding shotgun, and when I whacked her knee and pointed, she just slid her sunglasses down her nose, peered at the butterfly like it might be contagious, and said, "They're everywhere, Glo. A plague of them." After that, just like when you learn a new word and suddenly it's all over the place, I started seeing the blue butterflies everywhere I looked.

But then, I can't remember a time when I haven't looked for signs. It was not unusual for me, at age twelve, to tiptoe outside to our moonlit mailbox and fully expect to find within it (at midnight, on a random Tuesday!) a love note composed in Egyptian hieroglyphics or a grocery list scrawled in the shaky hand of the ghost of Boo Radley. Give me a fortune cookie, a Magic 8 Ball, a plague of blue butterflies, and I'll be sure to find in them some urgent message from the universe. Ask Carol: According to her, I'm a master of the Art of Arcane Communication but a complete idiot when it comes to the Writing on the Wall. What happened at Geek Camp? It was like that. I never saw it coming, not even for half a second.

That first magic blue butterfly stayed on the windshield of the Munch all the way to Dairy Queen. Carol's the one who came up with that: the Munch, as in LeBaron von Münchhausen. Carol's dad is a psychologist, so she's always talking about stuff like Münchausen syndrome. Carol has diagnosed half our class, and Münchausen syndrome is apparently what Sophie Allen has, because she's always feigning illness to get out of gym class. Carol says I'm pretty normal, but that I'm prone to hyperbole and should work on impulse control. Impulse control? Seriously? We'd been in the car for ten minutes and Carol had already texted her boyfriend, Oscar (pronounced "OH-scar" because he is, in Carol's words—and

inarguably—a Cuban Demigod) at least four thousand
times.

That's half the reason I couldn't wait to go to Geek
Camp: I was under obligation to check my technoparaphernalia at the door. According to the glossy brochure,
the idea behind Geek Camp is to provide Kentucky's "best
and brightest" rising high-school seniors with an early
taste of collegiate life. So you have to pick a major and
everything. I flirted with the idea of Forensic Science (too
gross) and briefly considered Theater Arts (too obvious),
but in the end I listed as my first choice the cryptically
named Secrets of the Written Word. The teacher—some
guy who called himself Dr. Weston A. Xavier—didn't even
provide a blurb for his class in the glossy brochure. Just
a title and a name, check the box here. The mysterious
blurb-lessness is what eventually won me over; I checked
the box, sent off my application, and hoped for something
wonderful. Dr. Weston A. Xavier didn't disappoint: Several weeks later I received a beautifully handwritten letter,
sealed with actual wax:

Dear Students,

I look forward to meeting each of you in June.
Before we begin, I must ask that each of you please
leave behind any personal computers, cellular
telephones, or any other means by which you might

find yourselves plugged in and tuned out. It's a
challenge, and I'm asking you to rise to it. We'll
operate on the honor system and I trust it will work.
By signing below, you enter into contract to abstain
from your gadgets for the duration of our four weeks
together. Bring a notebook and a writing implement
and you'll have all the tools you need.

Sincerely,

X.

"That is a freaking conspiracy right there," Carol had said when I showed her the letter. "X? He calls himself X?"

"Not even Doctor X. Just X."

"What a jackass," Carol murmured, fingers skating elegantly across her phone.

"There's nothing anywhere online about a Weston A. Xavier," I informed her. "It's a pseudonym, Carol, hello." I had to admit it: I was intrigued.

"Oh, well, excuse me," Carol said. "Mr. Pseudonymous X, of course. Mr. Pretentious Monogram. Sounds like some secret psychological experiment where somebody— some guy who's probably a *perv*, Glo—is trying to see if you all can function without the Vortex." The Vortex: that's Carolspeak for: TumblTwitFaceGram, which is basically where she lives, if you don't count brief forays to school, the ballet studio, and Dairy Queen.

"Who says the guy's a perv? He's probably just a

lonely J. Alfred Prufrock type who wishes he were teaching at Yale instead of some bush-league high-school academic camp."

"I'm just saying," Carol said, dangling the letter in my face. "Maybe this is your golden ticket and—oh, wait, oh, my God—if you can keep clear of your phone for a month, you'll win a chocolate factory in the end!"

I rolled my eyes. Conspiracy or not, I was looking forward to a break from the constant racket of modern technology. First of all, on the Vortex I'm more of a silent lurker than an active participant. Don't even get me started on the whole Pandora's box element—it poses a constant threat to my emotional well-being. Second, I have a bad habit of losing or breaking small, expensive items (my retainer, my contacts), so when I finally caved under my paranoid father's insistence that I go cellular in the name of Unforeseen Emergencies, I was forced to accept what is the mobile phone equivalent of a Jurassic-era dinosaur. The Unforeseen Emergencies? So far they haven't happened. So far the dinosaur has proven to be not a life preserver but a glorified umbilical cord connecting me to more sound and fury than I know what to do with. Third: It is physically impossible for me not to compose text messages in complete sentences in words that contain all their natural-born letters. By the time I have pecked out a response to, say, an urgent text from Carol ("omg did u hear?????????") in my own laborious, long-winded,

5

correctly capitalized, and carefully punctuated way ("No. Did I miss something? Tell me!"), Carol will have already sent like three more urgent messages in the interim. I can handle Latin, I can *amo amas amat* all day long, but I suck at text-ese and I'm constantly behind.

Anyway. I still had a few precious hours to go before surrendering to X and the Luddite life for four weeks. Carol and I ate our Blizzards in the Munch. The convertible top was rolled down, and the sunlight slanting through the trees was getting soft and syrupy in that way that makes you miss things that aren't even gone yet. This was our goodbye trip to DQ, because Carol was about to leave for her own summer adventure, a crazy-elite ballet school in New York City.

"You know," Carol said in her thoughtful voice, "in New York you can get a hoagie or a Rolex or whatever on the street at like four in the morning, but I don't think they have a DQ."

"Seriously?"

"Seriously. No Blizzards."

"Yikes. I might have to change my mind."

Carol shoved her sunglasses on top of her head, shot me a look. "Girl. You're not changing your mind. If you *even* let yourself get roped into that scholarship, I just—I just don't even know what. I might die."

"You're not going to die, and I'm not going to take the scholarship."

Carol narrowed her eyes, searching my expression for signs of half-assedness. "Do you promise?"

"I promise."

"Good. Because dude, the Plan abides. The Plan trumps the Scholarship. I will tattoo it on your face if I have to."

The Scholarship, the Scholarship. It's all anybody wanted to talk about, and I was so sick of talking about it I could've screamed. It's like this: If you get accepted to state government-funded Geek Camp, you also score an automatic free ride to the University of Kentucky, aka UK, aka the state's "flagship university." The idea, presumably, is that Kentucky needs to hang on to its geeks, the better to shake that whole shoeless, clueless, Kentucky-fried stigma. Which, you know what? Don't even talk to me about. I don't have a whole lot of patience with that bulsh.

Flagship. The word conjures pirates, skulls and crossbones, damsels in distress being forced to walk the plank. A romantic word that has nothing to do with the singular *un*-romance of going to college within a sixty-mile radius of the place where you grew up. The Plan? Now, the Plan was romantic: Carol and I were going to move to New York as soon as we graduated. She would be a dancer and I would be an actress and we would be broke, but our lives would be awesome and filled with mystery and intrigue. The details of the Plan were still fuzzy, but we knew it would involve a shared apartment strung with tiny white lights.

"Absolutely," I said. "The Plan abides."

Carol looked relieved. She poked at a chunk of cookie dough with her spoon. "So we're going to have to kick it old-school? Real letters, stamps and all?"

"Yep," I said. I was getting excited just thinking about it. Especially the stamps. Especially the part where Carol's letters and postcards would show up in an actual mailbox. Geek Camp was starting to become real, and a rush of nervous anticipation fizzed through my body.

"Okay," Carol said. "Just don't expect me to be all prolific. I'm going to hold you personally responsible when my ass gets carpal tunnel."

"I'm pretty sure your carpals are in your wrists, not your ass."

"Well. Then kiss my carpals, byotch."

We were cracking ourselves up, but what we were really doing was trying hard not to think about a whole summer without each other. The excitement I had felt a second before took a sudden slide into the realm of panic. It seemed impossible, unthinkable, that Carol and I would be separated (by eight hundred miles!) for the first time in the history of a friendship that began the day skinny little Carol from Alaska walked into sixth-grade language-arts class. Instead of behaving with customary New Girl humility, she acted like she owned the place. As with so many of

8

the things I love best in life, I hated Carol at first. A ballet dancer? From *Alaska*? She may as well have been a unicorn from the dark side of the moon. Later, I found out that not only did we share a portentous birthday (the Ides of March), but we were also both named for our grandmothers. Gloria and Carol: two totally geriatric names in a class that included no fewer than three girls called Kayla, all of them ridonculously magazine-beautiful. I took it as a sign, and the rest, as they say, is history.

Our friend the butterfly stowaway was still there on the windshield, folding and unfolding its marvelous blue wings. Call it hyperbole, call it whatever you want, but I'm telling you that it looked like it was waving, like it was going *goodbye goodbye goodbye*. Another sign from the universe, of course. It's important to pay attention to these things. We finished our Blizzards and cranked the seats back so we could stare up at the darkening sky for a while. We sat in silence as Carol's phone buzzed with the incoming messages of Oscar the Cuban Demigod. "I'm not even going to pick that up," Carol said, looking over at me and grinning. "That's how much I'm going to miss your Luddite ass."

I'm not a chronic crier or anything, but when I dropped Carol off in front of her house, it was all I could do not to bawl. We hugged each other like crazy and promised to write.

9

I hadn't been in the door for three seconds when my dad gave me that look he'd been giving me for days. The look said: *Have you packed yet? Why aren't you packing?*

If there's one thing I don't get, it's the business of packing in advance. I mean, if half the stuff you're going to need is the stuff you're wearing right now, or the stuff you're going to sleep in, or the stuff you'll need in the morning when you go to wash your hair and brush your teeth, then what's the point of packing it all away and getting it back out again? Ridiculous. But to appease my father, I shut myself in my room to commence "packing."

First I tuned my iPod to my Thinking Playlist so I could think. Next, in a move that I realized had become automatic, a bodily response to an actual physical urge not unlike the urge to yawn or pee, I checked the Vortex. After thinking for way too long about what might constitute a clever farewell, I finally settled on "Gloria Aaron Bishop is hereby headed into the Abyss. Parting is such sweet sorrow! Enjoy your summer, my lovelies." It was dizzying to think of everything I would miss—had already missed in the thirteen seconds that followed the shutting down of my laptop—but it was thrilling, too, and I couldn't wait for life at Geek Camp to begin.

In the end I decided to travel light and bring with me only two books: my prized copy of *To Kill a Mockingbird* and the Gloria Bishop Book of Ephemera. The first belonged originally to my grandmother Gloria, better known as GoGo. After she died and I inherited the Munch, I found the book stashed in the glove compartment beneath a bunch of lipstick-kissed tissues, an unpaid parking ticket, and a completely badass pair of cat-eye sunglasses. I recognized it as the same ancient copy that GoGo used to read to me from when I was little. When I was assigned to read the book for freshman English, I could actually *hear* GoGo's voice in my mind as I turned the pages. It's my favorite book of all time, ever, and finding GoGo's very own copy was like discovering the Holy Grail.

I guess now would be a good time to tell you more about GoGo, about how great she was, how unlike anyone else in this world, but it makes me too sad. That will have to wait. Instead, let me tell you about the book: It was filled with underlines and margin notes in GoGo's handwriting, plus—and this is the best part—a postcard from Munich, Germany, addressed to GoGo and signed by some mysterious person named Robert. Robert didn't have anything earth-shattering to say (*Hello from Weltstadt mit Herz! On to Hamburg Thursday. Back the first of June. Robert.*), but the handwriting is wicked cool and the stamp is even cooler.

Not only did GoGo's postcard from Munich provide a sign from the universe that "the Munch" was indeed the perfect name for my new ride, but it also became the first item in the Gloria Bishop Book of Ephemera. In the months that followed and especially since the arrival of the letter from X, the GBBoE has grown into a pretty epic collection of random stuff I've found, all of it featuring, in some way or another, the handwritten word. It was just like the butterflies: Once I started looking for it, the ephemera was everywhere. That very night, at the DQ drive-thru, Carol had handed me a rumpled dollar bill on which someone had printed in purple marker the words *TOO MUCH OR NOT ENOUGH?* Ha. The age-old question.

Before stashing the GBBoE in my duffel bag, I pasted Carol's dollar onto a page that already contained a list I had found stuck to the bottom of my cart at Target the week before:

Wipes
Diapers
Batteries
Q-tips
TP
Socks for P

And then my work was finished for the night. I fell asleep on top of the covers with the light still on, so maybe I dreamed this next part or maybe I made it up. Who knows?

My father, who makes a point of not entering my room except under extreme duress, came in around midnight. For the first time in years or maybe ever, he actually tucked me into bed. Before he turned off the light he leaned down, smoothed his palm across my forehead, and whispered in my ear, *I'm going to miss you around here.*

If I learned anything at Geek Camp, it's this: Missing people, and being missed, has an underrated charm all its own.

2

The Mad Hatter

GEEK CAMP isn't really called Geek Camp. It's called (very lofty) the Commonwealth Summer Program for Gifted and Talented Students. Which is hilarious, because I don't really consider myself Gifted or Talented. And much as it might be cool to attend GoGo's beloved alma mater (I can hear her now: "College is a privilege, honey. Not a right! Scholarships don't grow on trees! Count your blessings or count yourself a fool!"), I obviously did not apply to Geek Camp in hopes of securing a scholarship to the Flagship University of the State I Could Not Wait to Flee. I just wanted to spend the summer on a college campus—any college campus—if you want to know why I really applied. I wanted to live in a *dorm*. As I imagined it, dorm life promised what every only child wants: some approximation of the fascinating chaos that goes on in, say, Carol's house, which she shares with her parents and three brothers, and where there is never not mysterious boy-music blaring from somebody's room and where there is always, always tons of delicious food in the refrigerator. A dorm! I was totally enchanted.

My enchantment evaporated about three seconds after my dad and I arrived on the campus of Morlan College and pulled into the parking lot behind Reynolds Hall, where the female contingent of Geek Campers had been assigned to live for the summer. The lot was crammed with double-parked cars and parents and boyfriends and a nightmarish array of enough stuff to suggest that every single one of these girls had packed for an extended stay on Mars. In typical Gloria fashion, I had packed at the last minute and managed to cram everything I thought I'd need into one enormous duffel bag, which my dad was heroic enough to haul up the stairs to room 317. I followed with my favorite and indispensable pillow and my favorite and indispensable lamp (it's a cool lamp; it used to be GoGo's and it's made of an old Chianti bottle), because if there's one thing I cannot abide it's overhead fluorescent lighting of the sort I imagined to be indigenous to dorm rooms.

By the time we reached the door I was in full-on

Deer-in-Headlights mode, which my dad was smart enough to recognize as his cue to please let me take it from here. He gave me a sideways hug and planted a prepaid calling card in my palm. "Use the landline in your room," he told me. "And Gloria, honey"—and this next part I said along with him, because dude, it is his *refrain;* I can count on it at least once if not six times a day—"remember to use your head." He kissed my forehead as a reminder, like, *This is your head, Gloria, so use it,* and headed back down the stairs.

There are lots of advantages to being raised by a single father, and one of them is this: Fathers don't fool around when it comes to saying goodbye. They might look at you all swimmy-eyed and give you a sideways hug that promises they'll be back, but man, they have the good sense to know when it's time to *go*.

In addition to some pretty horrific fluorescent lighting, room 317 featured two beds, one of which had already been made up to within an inch of its life with an immaculate white comforter and a small mountain of throw pillows that appeared to have been arranged by a thirty-something design professional. I backed out of the room and checked the number on the door to make sure I hadn't accidentally barged into the headquarters of the dreaded resident adviser Jenny, a way-too-eager Geek Camp alumna and current Morlan student who for the past month had been cluttering my in-box with completely use-less "useful tips and reminders." Nope: 317. Home sweet home. I plugged in GoGo's lamp, tossed my bag on the unoccupied mattress, and took advantage of the chance to gawk at my roommate's stuff while she was out of the room.

On a shelf above her desk there were all these picture frames of the inane variety that I've been known to ridi-cule on principle, but which now actually helped me fig-ure out what was what. The biggest one featured a photo of my roommate (JESSICA, I presumed, from the letters written in puffy ink across the bottom of the frame) shak-ing hands with—no lie—Sarah Palin. JESSICA had on a tidy little suit and possessed the most dazzling set of white teeth I'd ever seen. A carbon copy of the same killer smile lit up other frames that provided me with photographic evidence of SISTERS (Jessica was apparently one of three), TRUE LOVE (Jessica was taller than her boyfriend), and BEST FRIENDS (Jessica and her cronies all wore the exact same ginormous sunglasses). My fingers actually twitched with the frantic desire to text Carol: *I am living with Barbie! Get me out of here!*

I was just starting to get self-conscious, to wish I had brought along something decent to wear or at least more of my personal library so I'd have something on my shelf to convey to the world who I was, when the actual flesh-and-blood JESSICA flounced into the room. She was on the phone, talking so fast I could hardly catch what she was saying.

"I know, right? She is literally right down the hall from me and I am not kidding he just dropped her off and he kissed her on the mouth in front of like fifty people oh my *God*. Wait hold on a sec."

My new roommate beamed and enveloped me in a hug that would suggest we had known each other for years. I'm usually not a fan of spontaneous and extraneous physical contact, but I was sort of moved by how the hug came so naturally to this girl, like affection itself was a language and she spoke it with easy, graceful fluency.

"Hi!" Jessica gushed. She was doing this intense stage whisper, presumably out of deference to the person on the phone. "I'm Jessica. Poli-sci. Kevin Donnelly is literally right down the hall this very second and I seriously come up to like *here* on him. It's insane! That's his girlfriend down the hall and she is so super sweet and they've basically been dating since birth and you are going to love her. Wait, hold on."

Then, back into the phone: "What? No. I was talking to my roommate. Wait. I'm sorry, what's your name again?"

I had looked away, trying to remember who Kevin Donnelly was, to concentrate on the bell his name was ringing. It took me a second to realize that the shift back to the stage whisper meant that Jessica was once again addressing me.

"Oh! Gloria. My name's Gloria. Hi." I did this nonsensical little wave.

Jessica reached out and squeezed my hand. She tilted the phone away from her mouth and stage-whispered, "Gloria, oh my God, we are going to have so much *fun*. Be right back. Oh, grab something from the fridge if you're thirsty."

As quickly as she had burst in, Jessica disappeared from the room, her voice back to its normal register but still going turbo-speed on the phone. I was just starting to feel despondent again when I turned to open Jessica's tiny refrigerator, the front of which was adorned with a sticker just like ones I had seen plastered all over a bunch of parents' cars in the parking lot: COAL COALITION, the sticker said. I had seen other stickers, too, almost identical but with a message clearly intended to appeal to the other team: SOL COALITION.

Now. I wish I could tell you that I was the sort of person who, upon being met with bumper-sticker proof of an environmental war being waged in the very state where I was born and raised—in the state where I was currently being expected to act as a freaking role model—might have actually devoted some thought and maybe even some allegiance to a side of said environmental issue, but the awful and embarrassing truth is this: Before I landed at Geek Camp, the business of mountaintop removal wasn't even on my radar. If Jessica's sticker registered with me at all in that moment, it was only vaguely. If I had to guess, I'd say I probably thought Coal Coalition was a band—an alt-bluegrass band, maybe, *huge* in outlying parts of the state but not in that grand sparkling diadem of Louisville, where bands of that ilk are clearly passé. *Coal Coalition.* I mean, it's a good name for a band, right? Featuring a sexily bedraggled lead singer with a come-hither look in his wounded eyes? Yes, I probably thought it was a band, because that's what you do when you're clueless: You apply your own narrow little realm of experience to everything you look at and touch.

It mortifies me now to say that I knew nothing then of an issue that was to become central to my thinking in the days and weeks that followed, but it's the truth: In that moment, I didn't think or care about the Coal Coalition, band or bandwagon. I was concerned only with Jessica's refrigerator, which was stocked with perfect rows of bottled Ale-8-One. Longnecks, my absolute favorite. Forget technoparaphernalia—if I'm addicted to anything in this world, it's Ale-8. Nectar of the gods, people. No lie. I took a long, gingery swig and immediately felt bad about the text I had wanted so desperately to send to Carol. Just when I had decided that Jessica and I had absolutely zero in common, that we would hate each other and there would be drama and the summer would suck and we would all disappear into gaping black holes, blah blah blah, there was a mini-refrigerator full of the freaking nectar of the gods. So maybe a soft drink shouldn't count as a sign, maybe and probably it wasn't anything to go hanging an opinion on, but in my mind it was proof of what Atticus Finch says about walking in Boo Radley's shoes. I forget the line exactly, but it basically comes down to what Walt Whitman said, too, in that poem I had to memorize for English class last year: People, man. People really do contain multitudes.

Incidentally, the weather was ridiculous. All week it had been the sort of mind-numbing hot that you'd expect from Central Kentucky in June, but that first day at Geek Camp was almost eerie in its cool, green gorgeousness. Jessica had left the window open, and the air that breezed into our room smelled like cut grass and warm skin, like possibility itself. Somebody outside was laughing, and the music of it made me impatient to be outdoors, to get my bearings and learn my way around campus, starting with the mail room.

I'd finally finished unpacking my stuff and was in the middle of wrestling sheets onto the mattress when one of those crazy blue butterflies sailed through the window, hovered for a few thrilling beats in midair, and swooped to a rest on the sill. With its wings pressed together behind its body, the thing looked for a second like a folded slip of paper, like a secret note passed in class, dark and thin as a razor blade. Carol was right: The butterflies *were* sort of scary. I was holding my breath as I inched toward the window for a closer look, but in that split second the butterfly lowered its wings and disappeared back into the bright afternoon.

And that's when I first saw him.

On the ground below, strolling across the courtyard toward Reynolds Hall, was this boy wearing—no lie—a floppy green top hat. He was apparently a stickler for detail, this boy, because tucked into a wide ribbon wrapped around the hat was a square of paper, à la the original Mad Hatter. À la Mr. I'm So Clever, which was obviously this guy's persona. He hadn't even walked twenty feet, I hadn't even really seen his face yet, and already my insides were doing a slow boil. If there's one thing I cannot abide, it's people who can't resist the temptation to call attention to themselves in the freaking noisiest way possible. There I was again, rapid-fire texting Carol in my head: *Remind me to tell you about the Mad Hatter, aka Mr. Narcissistic Personality Disorder.* So maybe I was staring. Okay, so I was staring, whatever, and the Mad Hatter looked up. He looked right up at me, grinned, and, twirling his hat toward the ground, gave a deep and infuriating bow. I spun away from the window and had to actually *sit down* because that's exactly the extent to which I felt like the air had been stolen from my lungs. Suffice it to say that, officially and irrevocably, I hated the Mad Hatter.

I must have still been in my stupor when somebody knocked on the door, because for one crazy second I thought it was going to be him. The Mad Hatter. I was all ready to ask what the hell that bow was all about, but when I yanked open the door, nobody was there. I could hear girls talking and laughing behind closed doors along the hall, but I didn't see anyone. I think I stepped on it before I saw it: a small white envelope, my name on the front, sealed in familiar red wax. Inside was an index card with a bunch of weird stuff scribbled on it:

0900
8884P697r
205

Normally I would have been six shades of thrilled by what looked like a code, a puzzle, something for my brain to wrap itself around, but I wasn't thinking clearly. The air seemed charged, electric, and I needed to get out into that cool green afternoon. I shoved the card into my pocket and took the stairs two at a time. Was I surprised by what I found on the ground outside? No, of course I wasn't surprised. The day, after all, had been full of signs and portent from the start. Here's the weird thing, though: It's almost like I *knew* that when I stepped outside I would find that piece of paper—the one from the Mad Hatter's top hat. Like a freaking calling card: *In this Style 10/6*. I shoved it into my pocket along with the message from X and went off to find something to eat. All of a sudden I was starving.

Morlan College's dining hall is called the McGrathskellar. It's in McGrath Hall, which is named after this guy Thomas McGrath, who freaked out and put a curse on the whole school a few hundred years ago. I learned this after following a huge herd of people into McGrath: Everyone was apparently going to a first-day-of-Geek-Camp ice-cream social (no lie: an *ice-cream social*) that I had somehow failed to get the memo about. People were walking around with Fudgsicles and Push-Ups and whatnot, and I was falling fast into Deer-in-Headlights mode again when Jessica ran up and linked her arm in mine. Her other arm was already linked with the arm of a girl who looked dead-on Michelle Obama, perfect biceps and all.

"Gloria! There you are. Sit with us! This is Sonya."

"Hey, Sonya," I bumbled, and with my free arm gave that same ridiculous wave from earlier. What was wrong with me? Then I made some brilliant observation like, "Seriously, I haven't had a Fudgsicle since I was like seven. I didn't know they still even made Fudgsicles!"

If Jessica and Sonya thought I was a moron, they were nice enough not to show it. Jessica marched toward an unoccupied corner table and parked us. I did a quick scan of the room: no Mad Hatter. Good. I relaxed a little bit and accepted Sonya's offer of half a Fudgsicle. The thing tasted exactly like first grade.

"So," Jessica said, giving the table an efficient little rap. "I just gave Sonya here a proper grilling—Gloria, you should be aware that Sonya is one of those pageant bitches—and now it's time for *us* to get to know each other, roommate. So far the only thing I know about you is that you've got all this gorgeous hair and you're just letting it go. As soon as we get back to the room I'm going to introduce you to my flatiron, but for now why don't you just give us the basic rundown. Where you're from and why you're here and all of that. Go!"

Suddenly paranoid about my hair, I gave Jessica and Sonya the basic rundown. I'd rather die than talk about myself out loud, so I sort of gave them the expurgated version. In return I learned that Jessica was also "one of those pageant bitches," having once been runner-up to Sonya herself, who was indeed the famous girlfriend of the famous Kevin Donnelly. Kevin Donnelly, the name finally clicked: the small-town dynamo who had recently achieved hero status as the country's number-one high school basketball player and most sought-after recruit of practically every college team in the nation, including his home state University of Kentucky Wildcats. To say that basketball is a religion around here would be to put it mildly. It would also be to put it wrongly, because as far as I can tell, in the annals of history, religion has been responsible for things like war and fallen empires, while the shared devotion to basketball among Kentucky's faithful has had the power to do near-impossible things like break down social barriers in my high school's cafeteria. I mean, I'd be hard-pressed right this second to give you a clear definition of a pick-and-roll or to tell you with any accuracy what a bank shot is, but I'll tell you this: My very own GoGo, who contained more multitudes than anyone else I know, was the most fanatical basketball fan I've ever met. I'm just saying. I haven't fully figured it out yet, but I'm convinced there's a recipe for magic in this whole basketball thing.

"I'm telling you, girls, this gig is getting real old real fast," Sonya was saying. "It's like he's cheating on me, but with a bunch of greasy white basketball coaches instead of another girl. If the boy's ego gets any bigger, I just don't even know what. Seriously, yall, when we go out it's like, *Oh excuse me baby, there's no room for me in this car because your big fat ego is all the time riding shotgun.* Whatever." Sonya shook her head, let out a long sigh, and rolled her eyes heavenward. I liked her immediately.

During Jessica's own rundown I learned that the two SISTERS from the photograph were twins, and that they would be juniors at Morlan in the fall. Jessica leaned toward us and lowered her voice to a conspiratorial

26

whisper as she revealed everything her sisters had told her about the curse of Thomas McGrath.

"So he was this biology professor, right? A botanist or something, from Europe or someplace. Anyway, he had all these crazy ideas about things, these revolutionary ideas that people weren't ready for or something, like envelope-pushing biological theories or whatever. Anyway, he got fired. They sent him packing, and that's when he put this curse on the school." Jessica paused for effect and to take a dainty bite of sherbet.

Sonya smirked, folding her beautiful arms across her chest in this girl-don't-you-bullshit-me pose. "What kind of curse?"

"Umm, the kind of curse where people start dying of the plague and the administration building burns down and all kinds of other weird stuff starts happening," Jessica intoned. "McGrath said he'd only lift the curse if they promised to bring his dead body back from Europe or wherever and bury him on Morlan College grounds." Her eyes were huge as she gauged our reaction, which was apparently not up to par. Not the type to lose a rapt audience, she changed tactics and went for the nonchalant: "Anyway, whatever, the guy's buried in some tomb right underneath McGrath Hall. Like maybe right under your *ass* right now this second, Sonya."

At this, Sonya climbed onto her chair in mock horror and let loose a truly impressive scream that made everyone in the room turn around and stare at us. It was one of those moments when I would have been thrilled if the floor had suddenly opened up and swallowed me whole. Sonya was amazing, though: She just waved, hollered, "How're yall doin," and climbed back down like nothing had happened. "Jessica," she said, "girl, you are more full of shit than my full-of-shit boyfriend. Let's get out of here, yall. Gloria, are you coming or what?"

I told Jessica and Sonya that I'd see them later and set off to find the student mailboxes. It was funny: I had hung out with my new friends for, what, fifteen minutes? Not a long time, and I liked them, I really did—I was even sort of in awe of their quick and generous affection for each other. Aside from brushing elbows on pageant podiums, they had known each other for exactly one morning and had already formed what appeared to be a fierce attachment. Equally awe-inspiring was their easy acceptance of me, even though I was clearly their polar opposite in a bazillion different ways. Anyway, I'm so weird this way, I really am, but even after fifteen minutes I was already feeling that familiar itch to go off somewhere and be by myself. I wanted to be alone long enough to let my mind settle down around all the new stuff it was suddenly carrying. The curse of Thomas McGrath, for instance, and the strange code on the message from X, which seemed, burning there in my pocket, to be a key to some treasure locked way down deep in the trunk of my imagination.

3

The Allegory of the Cave

I FOUND my mailbox, which was cool, even cooler because I already had mail! Seriously: The thrill I got at finding Carol's postcard waiting for me was not unlike the thrill I imagine people get when they win the freaking lottery. Carol had apparently mailed off the card (solid black on the front, with a caption that read KENTUCKY AT NIGHT) so it would arrive at Morlan before I did. In typical Carol fashion, the message was short and sweet (*Don't get too smart, Miss Smarty-Pants. Love, C.*), but it made me miss her. So far I hadn't missed my computer at all, and I was doing just fine without my dad, thank you, but without even a full day under my belt, I already missed

Carol. Most of all, though, I missed my *car*. I had all kinds of thinking to do, and I realized that my best thinking happens in the Munch, when I'm cruising River Road with the wind in my hair and the radio blaring.

The rest of my first day at Geek Camp passed in a flurry of obligatory and obnoxious get-to-know-you routines. After a dinner of Lucky Charms in the McGrathskellar ("Avoid the rectangular pizza and go for the cereal," Jessica warned me and Sonya, on the sage advice of her sisters), all 120 Geek Campers got corralled into the auditorium for orientation. God save me from orientations of any kind. Are they ever not a ginormous waste of everybody's time? So blah blah blah, all the resident advisers got introduced (Jenny was every bit as overly eager as I had imagined; Sonya mimed a gag), and then all the instructors got up to make their own introductions and let their students know where to find them at nine o'clock the next morning, when classes were set to begin. X was notably absent. In his place, the camp-director-slash-philosophy-instructor (who was actually wearing tweed in the middle of June!) stepped up to the mike and gave it a few experimental taps. A peal of eardrum-splitting feedback screeched through the room.

"Is this thing on?" Tweed Man inquired. Was he deaf? Deaf but stalwart, apparently: "Can you hear me in the back?"

In response, a paper airplane—yes, an actual paper

airplane, that quaint relic of days of yore—came sailing across a hundred rows of itchy red crushed-velvet seats and came to a silent rest at Tweed's feet. One hundred nineteen heads craned around to see who the expert pilot was. Well. Do I even need to say it? There was the Mad Hatter, of course, holding court in the back row. He grinned at his audience, reclined with his hands clasped behind his head, and propped his gangly-ass legs on the seat in front of him. People started laughing, of course. Somebody applauded. Everybody thought it was hilarious. I flailed back around in my seat, my cheeks on fire.

Poor Tweed. After clearing his throat and offering a valiant *ha ha,* he went on: "Those of you, um. Those of you who are signed up for Secrets of the Written Word will have already received direct instructions from Dr. Xavier as to where to meet for class tomorrow. Dr. Xavier regrets that an emergency called him away this evening, but he looks forward to meeting you in the morning. If you have questions, just, um. Just see me or talk to your resident adviser and we'll make sure to get everything squared away."

Jessica elbowed my arm and whispered, "Don't you think he's kind of cute, in a loser-ish sort of way?"

This, of course, was shocking and unacceptable. "What? Are you kidding? He's wearing a freaking top hat!"

Impulse control. I needed to work on it. Jessica looked

at me like I'd just screamed at the top of my lungs. "Not Paper Airplane Guy, silly. Philosophy Guy."

I took another look at Tweed, who, although orientation was over and people were starting to disappear in clusters out the door, was still standing there at the mike, looking sort of bewildered, like maybe he had something else to say but had forgotten what it was. "Jessica. Dude. No way. He's at least twice your age."

Back in room 317, Jessica and Sonya sat down to Vortex all the people who would be in their shared political science class. How was it that they had managed to acquire a freaking class roster, when all I had to guide me toward Secrets of the Written Word was a bunch of cryptic numbers? Anyway, they were getting kind of shrill, and I was getting tired, and X and his clever little caper were starting to get on my last available nerve. I had no choice but to bust out the one piece of contraband I had allowed myself: Indigo, my trusty iPod. Although X hadn't *expressly* banned iPods, I assumed they fell into the "gadget" category he had mentioned in his letter. Still, whatever, I can't live without Indigo and the underwater dreamworld I fall into each time I go into what Carol calls my "audiospells." (I've got this whole soundtrack planned out for my life, see. It's very serious business. My Make-out Playlist is stellar but unfortunately doesn't get ample play; my Driving Playlist is perfect for River Road top-down-in-the-Munch cruises; and of course my famous Thinking Playlist—smart-girl music: Regina Spektor, the Magnetic Fields, the Decemberists—is indispensable when it comes to things like packing, doing Latin homework, and deciphering X's obscure little code.)

0900
8884P697r
205

I stared at the numbers and letters until my eyeballs throbbed. I turned them around in my head every whichway, trying to ferret out some meaning: Were they dates? Did the numbers correspond to letters of the alphabet? Was 205 a room number? What was the story with that infuriating lowercase *r*? Underwater dreamworld swimming wasn't helping. Regina Spektor wasn't helping, either. I was starting to get a little panicky, so I closed my eyes and tried to see the numbers in my head, the way I used to be able to picture words in my head during middle school spelling bees. The way I would see the letters when GoGo and I would race to unscramble the Jumble words in the newspaper: I could just close my eyes and the jumbled letters would appear there, like my mind had snapped a photograph of them, and then the letters would arrange themselves into words that made sense. GoGo was always faster at solving the Jumble, but still. She was the one who taught me how to take pictures of things with my mind that way. That's just how GoGo was.

So X's freaky numbers were starting to float there, to jigsaw themselves together behind my closed eyelids, when somebody yanked an earbud out of my ear and snatched the card from my hand.

"Hey!" I yelped. "What're you doing?"

"No, what're *you* doing?" Sonya flung herself onto my bed and started studying X's card. "What's this?"

I gave Sonya and Jessica the expurgated version. I expected them to laugh, but they didn't. Instead, Sonya regarded the card with renewed interest while Jessica plugged in her famous flatiron. "This calls for an Ale and a makeover, girl," she said, opening the fridge with her foot. "Help yourself."

It took Sonya all of maybe three seconds to come up with a solution to the first set of numbers. "Well," she said. "Oh-nine-hundred hours. That much is obvious, right?"

"What, now?" Jessica asked as she clamped my hair in the jaws of her iron, no doubt frying it and ruining it forever.

"Oh-nine-hundred hours. That's military time. Nine in the morning. Wherever you're supposed to be, you need to be there at nine, which, hello, is when we all have to be in class, so no big mystery there." Sonya yawned, flopped onto her stomach, and started paging through a magazine back-to-front. "Now, I don't know what-all the rest of this nonsense is, so yall can try to figure out the next part. Gimme one of those Ales."

I just sat there gawking.

"What?" Sonya asked.

"How'd you do that?"

"Glo, girl, I'm not clairvoyant. I just come from a military family. It's the way we roll." Sonya went back to her magazine.

Glo. Sonya called me Glo, just like that. Nobody had ever called me Glo except Carol, and the nickname made me feel . . . what? It made me feel at home, I guess, although nothing was normal about this situation, nothing was *home,* especially not the business of having my hair fried to death and ruined forever by an actual straightening iron, a device I despise on principle. I love nicknames because you can't give them to yourself. They are these completely spontaneous, organic things, and you have to sort of *earn* them from other people.

"Let me see that," Jessica snapped. She picked up the card and sat down at her desk. "Yall be quiet for a second so I can think."

"Shhhh!" Sonya mocked. "Jessica's over there *thinking*!"

Jessica's thinking was interrupted by a knock on the door. Jenny, the dreaded resident adviser, poked her head in and grinned at us. "Hey, girls! I hate to interrupt, but it's past visiting hours. Sonya, time to head back to your room, okay?"

Sonya rolled her eyes and took her time rising from the bed. "Oh-kay," she mock-pouted, a stagy little dig for the benefit of Jenny, who didn't catch it. "Good night, Einsteins," she said over her shoulder as she made for the door, and then, as she squeezed past Jenny, she couldn't resist: "Are you going to tuck me in or what?"

Jessica missed the whole performance because she was still examining X's card. "Glo," she said (two Glos in one night!). "I think this is a library call number. I mean, I'm pretty sure that's what this is." Jessica pointed to the second row of numbers and letters.

I eyed the figures myself and felt completely stupid for not having made the connection on my own. I mean, I spend a whole freaking childhood in libraries and I can't recognize a Library of Congress identifier? Mortifying.

"Jessica"—I wasn't ready to call her Jess yet; these things take time—"I think you're right. Totally a call number." My heartbeat revved into high gear with the recognition of it. I had a huge urge to bust past Jenny and run straight to the library, wherever it was.

"Let's look it up," Jessica said, reaching for her iPad.

"No!" I said. "I mean, no thanks. I mean, I think we're supposed to figure all of this out in a different way."

"Are you sure?"

I nodded, still fizzy from the Ale and the solve. "I'm sure."

"Okay. Then I'm going to take a shower." She cocked her head and smiled at me. "Your hair looks good like that, you know."

After folding me in another of her easy-fluent hugs, Jessica gathered up a small mountain of shower gear and made for the bathroom down the hall. When the door clicked behind her, I stole a look in the mirror, and I was almost unrecognizable to myself. I'm not a huge fan of mirrors, and I've always regretted that my best features (my imagination, of course, and my memory—I live in constant and irrational fear of premature Alzheimer's) can't be seen from across a room, but the girl looking back at me was almost, *almost* pretty. I mean, I wasn't going to run right out and buy a flatiron or anything, but just for a second, just long enough for that one brief glance, I could sort of appreciate the appeal.

When I was in elementary school, I could never sleep the night before field trips. The sense of imminent adventure—the possibility of all the fantastic things that could happen the minute we got on the bus and the scenery changed—was almost too much for me to bear. The best field trip of all, the one that left me sleepless with anticipation every time, was the trip we took each year to the Children's Museum in Indianapolis. I loved everything about that museum and everything about the two-hour bus journey from Louisville. We always returned home after dark, and it seemed a strange and impossible thing, to emerge from a yellow school bus, dopey with sleep, and find your classmates and teachers standing there in the twilight. The out-of-context dark made everyone seem more human, somehow, like we were all in it together, whatever "it" was. I used to daydream about letting the bus leave the museum without me: I would hide in the Egyptian mummy exhibit until the museum closed, and then spend the night beneath the dinosaur bones. For as long as I can remember, I've just—God—I've just wanted so badly for something to *happen.*

When I woke from half-sleep to the jangle of Jessica's alarm clock, I recognized it right away: the night-before-the-museum feeling. I hadn't had it in years, and I was buzzy with it, could feel it tickling the back of my tongue. Shower, contacts, teeth brushing: Every necessary ritual seemed like a frustrating barricade between me and all the life I wanted to get busy living. I pulled on my standard first-day-of-anything uniform (indispensable blue sundress, jean jacket, indispensable yellow low-top Chucks and GoGo's shades), wound my wet hair into a lopsided knot on my head, and stuck a pencil through it to keep it out of my face. Breakfast and the obligatory Morning Meeting were excruciating, but finally, *finally,* the day was mine, and the library appeared in all its glory before me at the top of this impressive hill, right in the middle of campus. I don't know what I expected to happen when I walked in (trombones? a trapeze act?), but I was a little stunned by the quiet. A bored-looking student sat sentinel at the reference desk, and the pop of her gum echoed through the building as if we two were the only ones in it. She didn't even glance up from her magazine.

The note from X was now pasted into the GBBoE alongside the tag from the Mad Hatter's hat. I checked the numbers, just to be sure, and climbed the stairs to the second floor. Then I started in with the panicking. What if Jessica and I had gotten it all wrong? What if it wasn't a call number at all, and somewhere in some fabulous, arcane corner of the campus, class was carrying on without me? A sickening thought. When I reached the 800s, though, I found a boy sitting cross-legged on the floor, a book opened across his lap. He had the reddest hair I've ever seen, before or since. Like hard-core *vivid* red.

"Hi," I said.

The boy looked at me and flushed. "Oh, hey." He held up the book so I could see it. "Plato's *Republic*. Page 205: Allegory of the Cave."

I fought the urge to jump up and down and instead sat opposite the boy, who told me his name was Calvin. Calvin Little. "So, are you Chloe?" he asked.

"Who's Chloe?"

Calvin handed me an envelope identical to the one

that had been deposited beneath my dorm room door. "I found it stuck on page 205. It's addressed to Chloe Farris, Gloria Bishop, Mason Atkinson, and me. So I guess there are only four of us, and I guess you're Gloria?"

"You're smarter than you look, Calvin." As soon as the words escaped my mouth, I wished I could take them back. Calvin Little, I could tell almost immediately, was not the kind of person who should be greeted with sarcasm—which, I realized with a burn, is too often my customary Default Mode. I made up my mind then and there to henceforth handle Calvin with care. Words, man. They matter.

I tried again: "So what's it say? Let me see."

Calvin handed the envelope over. "I haven't opened it yet. I thought I ought to wait until we're all here. Right now I'm just trying to figure out what we're supposed to get from the Allegory of the Cave."

I studied the names on the envelope and hoped that Chloe and Mason would hurry up. "Any sign of X?" I asked.

Calvin shook his head. "Nope."

"The Allegory of the Cave. Isn't that the story with the fire and the shadows and whatnot?" It was all coming back to me from ninth-grade humanities class. Calvin looked at me and beamed. He was one of those really polite guys—the kind of guy who goes around beaming all the time and knocking the socks off of everybody's

40

moms with his good manners. I mean, he had his shirt tucked in and everything. He was wearing an actual belt. GoGo would've traded me for him in about three seconds flat.

"Yeah, that's it. Socrates tells this story about how these guys chained to the wall had only this one tiny slice of what they thought was reality. Like, they didn't know anything else, so they thought the shadows were, I don't know, the end-all." Calvin flushed again, like maybe he thought he had already done too much talking. Like maybe that was the most talking he'd done in a really long time. He seemed so embarrassed that *I* started to feel embarrassed. Man, bashful people really stress me out sometimes. I do better with people like Carol and Jessica and Sonya—people whose personalities take up so much space that I can just be free to listen, to sit back and take it all in and ruminate about it later. It's always a little alarming to be in the presence of a fellow observer.

Calvin got to his feet—he was way tall all of a sudden—and stretched. "I don't know," he said. "What do you think we're supposed to think?"

I thought about how Carol had started calling me a Luddite, and how now X was apparently comparing us—who could it be but us? Calvin and me and Chloe and Mason, whoever and wherever they were?—to a bunch of cave dwellers with a skewed view of reality. It occurred to me that Tweed Philosophy Guy could have been X in

41

disguise. I mean, come on: Plato? Anyway. That's when Chloe showed up.

Chloe Farris was tiny. Microscopic. She had one of those severe Louise Brooks–esque bobs, and her hair was so black it gleamed a spooky blue beneath the library's anemic lights. She was hauling a bag that was approximately three times as big as she was, and she dropped it to the floor with an emphatic thud when she saw me and Calvin in the 800s. When she opened her mouth, I expected a diminutive voice to go with her diminutive self, but her voice was remarkable: low and rich and scratchy, like maybe she'd had a few packs of cigarettes for breakfast. As if reading my mind, she extracted a pack of American Spirits from her ginormous bag and stuck a cigarette between her lips.

"I'm not going to light up, if that's what you're thinking," she said, blowing an impressive imaginary plume of smoke into the air. And then, squinting on the imaginary inhale: "I'm trying to quit, and I figure that half the reason I smoke is because I need a prop. I need something to do with my hands, you know?" Chloe tapped some imaginary ash onto the floor. "So what the hell, yall? It's like, *bonjour* and welcome to the wild-goose chase, right?"

Calvin and I introduced ourselves, and the three of us waited around for the elusive Mason Atkinson, who was either very late or very dim or both. Chloe smoked a couple of unlit cigarettes, and Calvin fretted some more over the Allegory, and about X, who we were all starting to believe was, at best, an allegory himself. We were considering taking our research outside when the sound of whistling came ringing up the stairs. If there's one thing I can't abide, it's whistling. The sound of whistling grates on my last available nerve. I mean, seriously: Who *whistles*? What kind of zip-a-dee-doo-dah crap is that?

The Mad Hatter. I couldn't freaking believe it. He came strolling across the library to where we had parked ourselves on some ratty leather couches. With one final, low whistle, he poured himself into an unoccupied ratty leather chair. "So," he said, "am I late?"

"Let me guess," I said. And then, because I couldn't help it, because I think maybe I had been rehearsing this line in my head ever since the episode with the window and the bow: "You're late because you were too busy believing six impossible things before breakfast?"

The Mad Hatter, aka Mason Atkinson, aka Jackass Extraordinaire, winked at me and nodded. "I believe the White Queen is responsible for that line," he said. "But I appreciate the sentiment all the same, my dear."

My dear? Who talks like that? Who goes around winking? I wanted to die. I wanted to fly right out of the room and knock the Mad Hatter on his egotistical ass on my way out.

"I'm Chloe," Chloe announced from her supine position on the couch. "This is Calvin and that's Gloria. Your hat is stupid. Would you care to open this letter from le Professeur?" Chloe frisbeed the envelope in Mason's direction and he raised an indolent hand to catch it in midair. A graceful maneuver, I had to admit.

Mason took his time opening our mail. "Breakfast served anytime," he read aloud. He looked up at us and grinned, waiting, I guess, for us to break into wild applause.

"What? Let me see," Calvin said. He was getting flustered.

"Breakfast served anytime," Mason repeated, tossing the card to Calvin. "That means we need to meet him at the Egg Drop. X marks the spot, right?"

"Wait. The what?" Calvin asked.

"The Egg Drop Café. It's this twenty-four-hour greasy spoon around the corner. Best milk shakes on the planet. Breakfast served anytime."

"And you know this *how*, exactly?" Chloe asked, squinting beneath her glossy bangs.

"I'm from here," Mason replied. "Born and raised." He got up from the chair and started sauntering back toward the stairs. Whistling. Again. When the rest of us just sat there looking at one another Mason stopped and turned around. "Are you coming?"

Well. Did we have a choice? We gathered up our stuff and followed the Mad Hatter down the rabbit hole.

4

The Egg Drop Café

THE STORY gets better from here. It actually gets pretty good. First, though, another story, because this one is permanently lodged in the back of my mind. Nobody has heard this story, not even Carol, and that's because the story is about Carol's brother Alex. He's the oldest of the four of them; it goes Alex (headed back to Alaska for college this fall), then Carol, then Hank (two years behind us in school), and then Paul (who, at fourteen, just recently became a real person). For as long as I care to remember, Carol's brothers have been a fact of my life. I'm around them all the time, and sometimes they get on my nerves, but I never really *think* about them, the way you never really think, say, about the bathroom wallpaper you've been staring at since you were born.

Last summer, that changed, and even though the change could fit into the space of three minutes, it's still the scene I see behind my closed eyes every night when I'm drifting off to sleep. It's still the image I conjure most often when I dive into underwater dreamworld to the accompaniment of my underused Make-out Playlist. It happened like this: Alex was giving me a ride home, which he had done at least a zillion times before. I was so at ease with him, he was so much like bathroom wallpaper, that we weren't even talking, which is how the six-minute ride from Carol's house to mine would usually go. I'm not sure what, exactly, made this ride different from any other, but in my mind it had something to do with the song Alex had going — this jangly sad song about a lighthouse. (The song is actually called "The Lighthouse"; I know this because it's on a CD, made especially for me by Alex, that appeared in my mailbox about twelve hours after the moment that became my go-to underwater dreamworld scene, but let's not get ahead of ourselves.) So cue the jangly song about the lighthouse. Then cue Alex, who, instead of screeching to the curb and letting the car idle while I skipped up to the door, cut the engine this time. Then he keyed the ignition enough to let the lighthouse song keep going, and then he shifted around to face me. "Gloria," he said. "Gloria, Gloria, Gloria."

It occurred to me that I rarely, if ever, heard Alex say my name out loud. Hearing it four times sent my stomach right off the high dive, *whoosh*. My heart was thrumming in my ears.

"What?" I said. (Because what do you say?)

Slow down and let the waves have their way now, went the song. God, that song!

"I have a secret to tell you," Alex whispered. Some shift had happened in his eyes—huge drenched brown eyes—like he might cry or laugh at any second, like his eyes were pools to go deep-end diving in, down, down, down. "Come here."

I came here. And Alex kissed me. He kissed me the way I imagined I'd always wanted to be kissed: both hands on my face. Without really noticing them, I had noticed his hands before—long and clean, like hands should be. He wore this wide leather cuff on his left wrist, and I could smell the leather, and his soapy skin, and I could smell the car engine as it ticked and cooled.

"There," Alex said. "Glad I got that out of my system." He smiled at me with this smile that was equal parts appreciative and mournful, embarrassed and proud. Because that was it—that was our three minutes. He was, after all, Carol's brother, and it couldn't be any other way. The next day the CD arrived in the mailbox, and the day after that I was back at Carol's, eating Doritos and marathoning *Friday Night Lights* and alternately fearing and hoping to God that when Alex drove me home he might give me a replay of that kiss, a kiss that put to shame all the other meager kisses I'd known in my life, all the inconsequential fumblings that those meager kisses led up to. But when Alex drove me home it was just like nothing had happened. We were friendly and silent and normal. Absolute wallpaper material. Which was fine. Which, really, was sort of a relief. That one kiss, though? It's mine to keep. The best secret anyone ever gave me.

That moment with Alex is worth telling not because it was the beginning or end of the world, but because it's always with me. I'll be in the Munch, say, stopped at a red light, and that jangly song will drift into my head and with it the image of Alex's lashes lowered against my cheek. The next thing I know, the driver of the car behind me will be honking at me to go. I'll be impulse-checking the Vortex and eye-rolling about everything everybody had for lunch, and from that unpredictable realm of daydream, Alex will appear unannounced. Alex, that Vortexless enigma, elusive and lovely in the most private corner of my mind.

Sometimes, when I go to Carol's and Alex isn't home, I'll take a detour on my way to the bathroom and sneak inside his room. I like to glimpse him when he isn't there: in the globe on his desk, the bass guitar tilted like a curvy girl against the wall, the books and CDs stacked in precise alphabetical rows on the shelves. The Strokes poster taped to the wall above the bed, and the bed itself, a tangle of sheets still twisted around the invisible shape of Alex's dreaming body. The globe, though. The globe is what kills me—the wishful, wistful boyishness of it. I've thought of that stupid globe an inordinate number of times, if you want to know the truth, and always it puts this awful ache at the back of my throat. It's weird, how *thinking* about Alex is the thing, the treasure. I think if I spent half the time actually being with him that I spend thinking about him, it might somehow break the spell.

So I was thinking of Alex while Chloe was railing against cell phones at the Egg Drop Café, this anomalous little hole-in-the-wall where you could get burgers and Tater Tots but where also—totally random—you could order moo goo gai pan or hot and sour soup. This tiny Asian woman banged a plate of fries on our table as the Black Eyed Peas thudded out of the jukebox in the corner. By way of random decoration, the jukebox had a paper fan taped to it. The four of us—Chloe and me and Calvin and Mason—were crammed into this greasy booth in a configuration that would become the norm for us: me on the inside across from Chloe, Calvin on my right across from Mason. It was good having the Mad Hatter on the diagonal, where I could avoid eye contact if necessary. Despite his having successfully led us the three blocks from campus to the Egg Drop, where X's next directive was indeed waiting for us behind the counter, I was still wary of him.

"Look at that guy over there," Chloe said, nodding in the direction of this completely harmless-looking boy, circa our age, who appeared to be enjoying a milk shake with his girlfriend.

"What about him?" Calvin asked. He gave a furtive little glance and shifted in the booth. You could tell he didn't have it in him to go staring at other people, much less talking about them.

"He's been over there with his face in his phone since we got here," Chloe said. She was smoking her straw and waving it around. "That poor girl just keeps yammering on and on, and he's not listening to a word she's saying. He's probably over there playing a video game or some shit."

Mason craned around to look. "So? Can you hear that girl's voice? Fingernails on a chalkboard, man. I'd rather text her than talk to her, too."

Chloe elbowed Mason in the ribs. "*So,* it just proves what I'm trying to say, which is that phones are this generation's cigarettes. It's an addiction, dude, but it's not about communication, just like it's not about nicotine. It's about holding something in your hand that makes you feel important. It's about props. Drama. I'm just saying."

Calvin cleared his throat. "Actually, it's about dopamine."

"Dopamine," Mason repeated. "Like the band?"

Dopamine: The word drifted in my head and I tried to seize onto it, but I kept coming up with Dramamine, à la GoGo's old motion sickness remedy.

"Not the band, the neurotransmitter," Calvin went on. "Chloe, when you take that first drag on a cigarette, you get a little shot of happy, right?"

"*Oh,* yeah," Chloe said. "But Calvin, sweetheart, don't be all yanking my chain. I'm trying to quit, remember?"

Calvin nodded and blushed. "So that little shot of happy, that's dopamine, telling your brain to be content. And every time you get a text message, or new Facebook updates, or an e-mail in your in-box, or whatever, that's another little dopamine shot, bam, right to your brain. The more texts you get, the more your brain craves them. It's what addiction's all about." Calvin paused to gulp from his milk. He glanced up at us and seemed surprised that we were listening, waiting for him to go on.

"So, Calvin," I asked. "What are you addicted to?"

"I'm addicted to these fries," Mason interrupted. "Pass the ketchup?"

I extracted the ketchup from its sticky chrome harness and banged it in front of the Mad Hatter. I shot him a midlevel death glare.

"I don't know," Calvin answered. "I mean, I don't think I have any addictions. I don't have a cell phone or a Facebook account, so it wasn't hard for me to give those things up when X asked."

Chloe gave Calvin a wide-eyed stare. "Calvin. Oh, my God. Are you a Bible-beater?"

Calvin laughed and picked at his fries. "Actually, I'm embarrassed to say I've only been to church like twice in my life. I'm just interested in what makes our minds want what they want, that's all."

My heart gave a sudden lurch of worry and affection for Calvin. "I'm addicted to Ale-8," I blurted. To illustrate, I downed the rest of my bottle. "I also think I'm addicted to the night-before-the-museum feeling."

Everyone stared and waited for me to go on, so I grabbed a fry from our shared pile and leaned back in the booth, all blithe nonchalance.

"Um, care to elaborate?" Chloe said.

"Yeah," Mason chimed in. "Do tell." His eyes locked with mine for a dizzying fraction of a second.

So I tried to explain to them the night-before-the-museum feeling, but of course that's not the kind of thing you can really explain. God, there's nothing worse than trying to stick words onto something really important and knowing that what's coming out of your mouth sounds like total nonsense. The whole time I was talking, I was aware that the Mad Hatter had cast his eyes downward toward his plate, that he wasn't really listening to me, that he was chewing his straw and getting bored. Then he surprised me. He was always doing that—surprising me.

"Well, Gloria," Mason said (what is it with the sound

of my name spoken aloud?), "It seems like maybe you've got a Grecian Urn complex." He flicked his eyes back in my direction and parked them on my face.

"Excuse me?" I snapped. I stared back, daring him to look away first.

"Wait," Calvin said, leaning forward in his brow-furrowed, get-to-the-bottom-of-this pose. "Is that like an Oedipus complex or something?"

I shot Calvin a look. "Wait a minute, dude—who says I want to bang my mom and kill my dad?"

Chloe snorted. "Oh, my God, yall. Don't make me laugh when I'm drinking. That totally went up my nose."

I folded my arms across my chest and waited for the Mad Hatter to go on. After a prolonged performance of polishing off the rest of the fries and wiping his hands on the remains of a shredded napkin, he lifted a finger and started nodding at us, like, *Oh, hold on a second, I will enthrall you with my infinite wisdom as soon as I'm done masticating.* Seriously: My hatred of him was starting to become epic.

"Grecian Urn, as in John Keats," Mason finally declared. "X's clue. Didn't you guys look at it?"

After Mason had collected it from the to-go counter, X's latest clue had gotten lost in our hurry to fuel ourselves. It lay there in the middle of the table, getting soggy around the edges.

"Wait a minute, did you read it without us?" Calvin wanted to know. "Okay, new rule: Nobody opens the letters until we're all together."

"We *were* all together, bro," Mason said. "You all just weren't paying attention. This one's not exactly mind-blowing, anyway. Like I said: John Keats. 'Ode on a Grecian Urn.' I had to read it for AP English last year."

Chloe picked up the letter and started reading out loud. When she got to the part about *heard melodies are sweet, but those unheard are sweeter,* Mason interrupted her.

"See, Gloria? Right there. There's your museum feeling. It's like, for you, anticipating the museum is better than actually going to the museum." He stared at me, waiting. "Am I right?"

"No, you're not right," I said. But of course he was right. I was seized by the irrational worry that he could see straight into my brain, could maybe even steal a glimpse there of Alex, my own secret personal private Alex, turning to face me in the car. "You're wrong. I loved that museum."

"Oh-*kay,*" Chloe broke in. "How about you two discuss that amongst yourselves later. Right now I'm going to finish reading this hideous poem, and then maybe Calvin can tell us where to go from here. Sound like a plan?"

"Keep reading," Calvin said. "I'm listening."

Chloe read the rest of the poem, which even

Calvin couldn't wrap his brain around, and then our server showed up with a bill and a plate of fortune cookies.

"Who's got money?" Mason said. "Chloe?"

"Shit, I forgot my wallet," Chloe replied, rummaging in her bag.

"Dude. You've got a whole arsenal of crap in there, but you don't have any money?"

"Shut up, Mason. Gloria, what about you?"

I shook my head and looked at Calvin, who was already quietly plucking bills from his wallet. "Bank of Calvin, open for business," he muttered. "Since when does it cost fifteen dollars for four people to share some french fries?"

I reached across Calvin to grab a fortune cookie. Fortune cookies are possibly the grossest things on earth, but I love them.

Never miss a chance to keep your mouth shut.

"Hey Mason," I said. "I think I got yours." I handed over the message and beamed. Mason flashed me a smirk, cracked open his own cookie, and read aloud, "Too many people volunteer to carry the stool when it's time to move the piano."

"Okay, that one's obviously mine," Calvin said. "Chloe, what'd you get?"

Chloe bit into her cookie and frowned. "Are these things ever not stale?" She chewed as she regarded her fortune. "Suck! I got the piano one, too."

Mason reached for the last cookie. "This one must be yours, then, Gloria. Why don't I read it for you?" He made a great show of breaking the cookie and extracting the message within. A slow smile spread across his face.

"What's it say?" I asked. "Give it here."

"This one is definitely yours," Mason answered. He passed it across the table and, like your average seven-year-old, yanked it away when I made a move to grab it. When he finally relinquished it, here's what I read:

Those grapes you cannot taste are always sour.

Before I could give him a proper glare, the kind of glare that would say, *I am not at all interested in your grapes, jackass,* Mason rose from the booth, stretching luxuriously.

"Shall we?" He yawned.

"Yes," I said, "We shall."

We trudged back to campus in silence. The Grecian Urn had landed us at a dead end, so we decided to stop on a stretch of velvety green lawn in front of the administration building and think things over. In the middle of the lawn stood this huge sycamore tree, the biggest I've ever seen, and from an impossibly high branch hung a rope swing, anchored at the bottom by a single slab of wood. The Mad Hatter broke into a sprint and did a flying leap onto the swing. His top hat sailed from his head as the swing swept him in a wide, graceful curve across the lawn.

Soon he was spinning himself dizzy and barking the kind of genuine laughter I hadn't heard or experienced myself in way too long. You couldn't *not* smile at that kind of unadulterated joy.

Chloe hooted a congratulatory whistle and clapped her hands as we made our way toward the tree. "Very nice," she laughed.

Mason took a bow and collapsed on his back in the grass. Without the hat, he looked almost normal: sweaty strands of unruly dark hair stuck to his temples, cheeks flushed with laughter and punctuated by dimples I hadn't noticed before. His eyes, those alert blue accusers, seemed . . . I don't know. Kinder somehow.

"Who's next?" Mason asked, breathless.

Chloe settled herself down with an unlit cigarette and X's Grecian Urn clue. I joined her on the grass and started to paste our cookie fortunes into the GBBoE, and Calvin dove for the swing, where he stayed, swaying in great arcs with his eyes closed, for an impressively long time.

"Calvin's in thinking mode," Chloe said, smiling. "Let's leave him alone." She glanced over at my work. "Do you seriously carry a glue stick around with you everywhere you go?" she asked.

"Yep," I nodded. "What about you? I'm guessing there's something in that bag besides your placebo-smokes."

"Everything and nothing," Chloe answered. "Do you need any Pez?" She dug into her bag and came up with a Hello Kitty Pez dispenser. "Three-D movie glasses? Dr Pepper Lip Smacker?"

I smiled at her. Definitely a kindred spirit. "No, thanks. I'm good."

"I like those shades," Chloe said. "Are they vintage?"

And so I sat there on that lawn and told Chloe about GoGo. I was surprised at how easily the words tumbled out, like I had been waiting forever for someone to ask me about my grandmother. And Chloe, she listened. She didn't interrupt me or break in to tell me about *her* grandmother or try to lay claim to my sadness by co-opting it with some sad story of her own.

"Your GoGo sounds awesome," Chloe said. "I was totally born into the wrong generation."

Chloe went on to tell me about her obsession with France, her adoration of Louise Brooks and Charlie Chaplin, her love of silent movies, her collection of vintage flapper dresses and costume jewelry. "If I could time-travel, I totally would," she sighed.

How long had it been since I'd talked with someone this way? Not just say words out loud to enjoy the sound of my own voice, not just pick the most convenient witty thing to say, but really talk, and listen back? It seemed like such a small thing, but I seriously couldn't remember the last time it had happened. The stretch of time we found ourselves in, the swath of sunshine warming our hair and the backs of our necks, seemed almost criminal. It was hard to shake the itchy feeling that we were supposed to be somewhere, that we were under the watchful eye of some in-charge person who could admonish us or give us a test or arrest us or send us packing back to our parents at any moment. Our freedom felt foreign and exhilarating. There was Mason, dozing as the grass breezed against his face. There was Calvin, leaping off the swing and crouching to examine something on the ground. I glanced around at other Geek Campers crisscrossing the lawn: laughing, hurrying, phones pressed to their ears. They seemed remote from the four of us. Part of me envied them—they looked full of purpose, engaged in something we were missing, something I didn't want to miss—but a greater part of me felt glad to be apart from them, and protective of this mission I found myself on with Chloe and Calvin and Mason. It was ours now, and it felt somehow too secret or sacred a thing to share.

Calvin approached us so gently that I didn't hear him. He knelt next to Chloe and me and opened his cupped hands. There, on his palm, was a blue butterfly. It seemed completely at home in his hands, in no hurry to fly away.

"Look at that," Chloe breathed. "Beautiful."

I asked Calvin what kind he thought it was, and he shook his head. "I don't know," he said, "but it's pretty incredible."

Yes, we agreed. It was.

5

Lepidopterology

"HE DIDN'T *give* a reason, Mom," Jessica gasped into the phone. She was pacing the floor of room 317 and her face was bloated with tears. When she picked up the TRUE LOVE picture frame and hurled it against the wall, I took my cue to leave and started backing out the door I'd just opened.

"No, don't go," Jessica pleaded, enveloping me in a hug and pressing her teary face against my cheek. "Stay!"

God. Talk about being held hostage. I surrendered to the bed and tried to absorb myself in one of Jessica's magazines. For fifteen excruciating minutes, I was privy not only to the gory details of Jessica's apparent breakup ("He sent me a *text*, Mom!"), but also to way more information than I'd ever want or need about the now-defunct romance ("I can't ever get my virginity back, not ever!"). I guess it shouldn't have come as a surprise, but it completely blew my mind that (a) Jessica ostensibly had a bona fide active sex life; and (b) she would discuss it in detail—with this air of total nonchalance and collusion, no less!—with her mom. I silently thanked God that my father rarely dared to trespass in my room, much less the private recesses of my heart. I made a mental note to thank him.

"Come and get me," Jessica begged her mother. "Please just come and get me. I can't stay here!"

At this, I opened my eyes wide and, shaking my head, mouthed the word *no*. "Hang *up*, Jess!" I hissed. She trained her red-rimmed eyes on me and gave a flustered nod.

"Okay," she said into the phone. "Okay, call me when you get close." She hung up and folded herself into a fetal position on the bed. The sobbing that ensued was awful. Jessica's whole body was heaving, and she was having trouble catching her breath. I didn't know what to do—I had never felt that way about a person, and I was weirdly, selfishly jealous at having never been there before. I didn't know anything about the short guy in the demolished picture frame and I didn't care to know, but whoever he was, Jessica loved him. Not just TRUE LOVE, either, but the real-deal kind of love that knocks your heart inside out. That much was obvious. I let Jessica downshift from full-on sobs to intermittent sniffles before I sat down next to her. I put a tentative hand on her shoulder.

"Jess?"

"Yeah?" Jessica gulped, wiping away snot with the back of her hand.

"You need to call your mom back, right now, and tell her to turn around. You're not going anywhere, okay?"

"I can't stay here." Jessica cried, turning away from me and burying her head beneath a pillow. "I can't!"

I didn't know what else to do, so I picked up our anti-quated dorm-issue phone and punched in some numbers. "We're having an emergency," I announced. Thirty seconds later, Sonya appeared at the door.

"What's going on?"

"Breakup. It's bad."

"Oh, shit." Sonya sighed. She crossed the room and stretched herself alongside Jessica's crumpled form on the bed. "Girl, start talking."

With great effort, Jessica unfolded herself and told Sonya everything. All through the story, Sonya listened carefully and nodded. She rubbed Jessica's back and was all support and comfort until Jessica came to the part about how her mom was currently en route to Morlan to pick her up. At that point, Sonya got up and started looking around the room.

"Jessica, where's your phone?"

"What?" Jessica asked, totally out of it.

"Gimme your phone a second. Is this it?" Sonya raised her eyebrows in inquiry, holding aloft a pink iPhone. Without waiting for an answer, she started scrolling around on the screen until she found what she was looking for. She looked over at me and mouthed the words *It's ringing.*

"Sonya, wait—" Jessica tried, failing.

"Hello, Mrs. Dixon?" Sonya cooed brightly. Immediately I could see why this girl rocked the pageant circuit. She was a natural. "This is Sonya Henderson, Jessica's friend?"

At this point we could hear the frantic, high-pitched warble of Jessica's mom's voice through the line. You could just imagine her at the helm of some SUV, barreling down the Mountain Parkway in hot pursuit of her fragile daughter, totally jacked up on the adrenaline that comes with Being Needed. Jessica was buried once again beneath her fortress of throw pillows—I couldn't tell if she was laughing or crying, but her shoulders were shaking—and I myself was doubled on the opposite bed with a hand clamped over my mouth, trying not to laugh my ass completely off.

Sonya held the phone away from her ear and, rolling her eyes, made a *quack-quack* motion with her hand to let me know that Jessica's mom wasn't going to shut up anytime soon. "Jess," she whisper-demanded, "what's your mom's name?"

"Diane," came the muffled response. Jessica was definitely laughing.

"Diane," Sonya said sweetly. "May I call you Diane? May I interrupt for just a second, Diane? Can I have your attention for just a minute?"

It was too hilarious. My eyes were watering from the effort of not laughing out loud. By the time Sonya switched from trying to prohibit Diane's imminent arrival to lecturing on the ills of Helicopter Parenting ("There've been studies, Diane—I promise that you are not doing your daughter any favors!"), I had to leave the room and stumble to the bathroom so I wouldn't pee in my pants. By the time I returned, Sonya was off the phone and the crisis appeared to have been averted. My friends were locked in a hug and Jessica managed a weak smile. "Thanks, girls," she said.

"That's what we're here for," Sonya replied. "Next time, call me *before* you call your crazy-ass mama."

"So." Jessica sniffed. "Gloria, how was your day?"

As much as I wanted to, I was unable to tell Jessica and Sonya about my day. I mean, I didn't lie; I just told them it was fine and changed the subject. First of all, it all felt too strange, like the students assigned to Secrets of the Written Word had fallen through the cracks or slipped through some loophole. The four of us had spent the entire three hours of the afternoon session trying to glean the whereabouts of X's next clue, but we never found it. We hung out in the college's official art museum (reasonably, Chloe had reasoned that there might be an urn in there) and scoured the library again, but we never got close, each of us sensing that we were way off the path. Were we failures? No, I don't think so. We hadn't found X, but we suddenly knew a lot about Plato, even more about John Keats ("Born on Halloween," Mason informed us, grinning. "My kind of ghoul"), and we were starting to know a lot about one another.

I felt weirdly protective of Chloe and Calvin, and even of the Mad Hatter himself. Carol says I do this all the time: I *compartmentalize* my friends, she says. An obnoxious habit, I know, but I can't help it. I was already overthinking my new friendships, the part of myself that each of them hinged on. What if Sonya and Jessica thought Chloe was weird? ("That must mean *you* think Chloe is weird," Carol would tell me, but of course I don't think Chloe's weird!) What if Chloe thought Sonya and Jessica were bitches? ("That must mean *you* think they're bitches"—but I don't!) And so on and so on in this ridiculous psycho loop. I swear, sometimes I wish my brain had an off switch. Already I was worrying about how my Geek Camp friends would or wouldn't get along with my Real Life friends once I got home. Sonya and Carol? They would kill each other! It's part of what freaks me out about the Vortex: Your school friends get all mixed up with your neighborhood friends or your friends from the swim team or your friends from last summer's trip to the beach. It's like I'm a little kid who gets all uptight if her macaroni touches her broccoli on the plate. Same thing exactly: I get uneasy when my friend-groups touch on the plate. Carol would tell me to stop worrying so much about everybody else and worry about my own bizarre self instead, but I can't help it. It's like all these people are just too . . . dear to me, or something. It's ridiculous, how people become dear to me in, like, five minutes. But they do. They did.

That night, after our room had gone dark and still, Jessica's voice stirred me from sleep. "Glo?" she asked. "Are you awake?"

"I am now."

"Oh, sorry," she whispered. "Go back to sleep."

"No," I said. "What is it?"

Her face was turned toward the wall. "You know what's weird?"

"Hmm?"

"I always thought it was stupid, that word *heartbreak*. I mean, it's not like our hearts are made of pink construction paper and you can just rip them in half, right?"

I didn't know what to say.

"But my heart," Jessica continued, "it really,

physically hurts me. It aches, just like heartache, just like that word I've always thought was dumb and didn't make any sense."

"I believe you," I said. And then, because it occurred to me I didn't know, hadn't even bothered to ask: "What's his name?"

"Brandon," she answered, and the name made something in her voice fall apart.

"Brandon," I repeated. I thought about GoGo, how when she died I felt like my heart had hollowed out and abandoned me, and the hole it left behind was full of ache. I didn't say that to Jessica, because this was her ache, not mine. This was a totally different thing. "Think of it this way," I said, scanning the dark ceiling for wisdom. "The way you're feeling right now really sucks. It's going to suck for a while, so you should just go ahead and let it suck."

Jessica sniffed. "Yeah," she said quietly.

"But dude, you can't let it suck for too long. Sooner or later, you've got to get up and be like, 'Hey, man, you know what? I've *loved* somebody. I've been loved by somebody. Nobody can ever take it away from me, and it's part of who I am now.' You've just got to chalk it up to hard-earned experience and own it and keep going and hopefully love somebody else one day."

Jessica was quiet for a long time. "I don't want to love anybody else," she finally whispered.

"I guess that's fair," I said. "For now, that's fair."

My mind was still locked on to GoGo, how I had known her death was coming, how it had made me feel sick because I couldn't stop it. I had dreaded it for so long, had worried for so long that I would just break away into pieces and die with her when she went, that when she did finally go, the feeling that came over me was this weird relief—a relief so huge and palpable that it shamed me. Wasn't I supposed to be sad? Relief seemed the opposite of what I should be feeling, but I wasn't relieved that she had died. I was relieved that the dreading was over, and—God, weird as it seems—I was relieved that I hadn't died with her. The sun came up the next morning, and I was still alive, more alive than I had been before.

"Jess?" I asked, tentative.

"Yeah?"

"Is part of you relieved?"

"What?"

"Never mind," I said. "Stupid thing to say."

Jessica gave a long sigh. "I don't know," she answered. "I mean, I guess in a way I knew this was coming. He's going to Wake Forest in the fall."

"So maybe better now than later?"

"Who knows," Jessica answered. "I'm exhausted. I'm exhausted and I cannot *believe* he has already changed his Facebook status to Single."

I rolled my eyes at the ceiling. "You don't need his Single ass, Jess," I said.

"Thank you." Jessica giggled. "That's more like it. Goodnight, Glo."

"Goodnight."

Then, two seconds later, just as dreamworld started swirling in: "Glo?"

"Mmm?"

"How come you haven't mentioned your mom?"

Shit. Where did *that* come from? I mean, really. I don't know what it is with people. A kid gets lost in a department store, and it's all, *Honey, where is your mother?* Some celebrity is naked and covered with obscene tattoos and shooting up heroin and eating livestock onstage, and it's *Doesn't that guy have a mother?* So Jessica, out of clear blue nowhere, wanted to know about my mother. Unbelievable.

"Well," I said, "there's not really anything to talk about. She left a long time ago."

"Oh," Jessica said. She said it like she was apologizing. She shifted around, facing me now. "Do you miss her?"

I thought about it for a second. There's only one right answer to that question, after all, or at least there's only one answer that people want to hear, but the truth is that sometimes the truth gets fuzzy. Loving my mother and missing her, I realized, were maybe two different things.

"Have you ever seen one of those lightning ball things?" I asked. "You know, those balls where the lightning's inside, and you can move your hands around on them and your hair gets all staticky and stands on end?"

"Yeah."

"Yeah. Well, okay. Close your eyes and imagine being inside one of those balls."

Jessica giggled. "Okay."

I squinched my eyes shut, too, because this was a hard thing to explain, and I wanted to get it right the first time so I could get a lock on the subject from here on out. "Being inside a lightning ball is sort of what it feels like to be in a room with my mother. I mean, it's gorgeous in there, right? Really exciting and colorful? Sure it is. But man, more than anything else it's just really freaking dangerous."

When Jessica opened her eyes they were shining in the dark.

"So yeah," I said, trying to keep things upbeat. I didn't want Jessica getting all upset on top of her own heartbreak. Isn't that always the way, though? The facts of a person's circumstances are usually way more upsetting to other people than they are to the person in question. When it's your own life, you just keep going, you just do what you have to do, it's just how things are, the way you have to roll. No matter what, there's always somebody who has it about ten million times worse than you do. "Yeah, sometimes I miss her, but I don't really miss life in the lightning ball, if that makes sense."

"That makes sense," Jessica said.

"Now, my grandmother? My grandmother GoGo?"

"Yeah?" Jessica's voice was drifty, sleep-tinged.

"I miss GoGo all the time. Most minutes of the day, more or less."

Jessica was fast asleep. I stared at the ceiling until I couldn't keep my eyes open any longer.

I woke early the next morning to find Jessica's bed unoccupied. A note was taped to the alarm clock: *Gone for a run. C U at breakfast. J.*

Stirred by that familiar longing for magic, I felt compelled to check my campus mailbox before getting dressed or eating or doing anything else. I stuck Jessica's note into the GBBoE, put on my glasses, yanked a hoodie over my pajamas, and took off barefoot across the courtyard. Everything was quiet: grass still silvered with dew, birds making break-of-dawn racket in the trees. For that moment, the morning was all mine, hushed and lush and sparkling. It wasn't lost on me, is what I'm saying. That crazy John Keats had gotten all up in my head, and suddenly the world looked different.

The campus mailboxes were old-school: little

numbered rectangles, each with a tiny keyhole and a glass front, so that you could peer in and see right away if there was a letter slanted in there, waiting to be opened. I had a perverse appreciation for my little mailbox key, and when I walked into the stuffy mail room and glimpsed the promising slant of something in my box, my heart cartwheeled with perverse glee. I keyed open my box—even the click of the lock was satisfying—and pulled out not one but two things: a stampless blue envelope addressed to me in precise, angular handwriting, and a CD-shaped square, wrapped in brown paper and graced by the all-capital block letters that I knew by heart to be Alex's.

I had to fight the urge to sit right down on the mailroom floor and tear open my treasures, but this was my forte—prolonging the moment for as long as possible, savoring the anticipation, rocking the Grecian-Urn and the night-before-the-museum feelings, all of that—so I ran all the way back to a still-quiet room 317, equipped myself with Indigo and my Thinking Playlist, and sat cross-legged on the bed with my loot spread out before me. The CD-shaped package was already sending my heart into overdrive, so I shoved it under my pillow and vowed to myself that I wouldn't open it until after dark. First of all, it was a nighttime sort of item, and second, this way I could *anticipate* it all day long.

The mysterious blue envelope turned out to contain

its own thrilling gift: a drawing of a blue butterfly, painstakingly rendered in varying shades of colored pencil. It was almost more beautiful than the real-life blue butterflies outside, and the loveliness of it brought that familiar, achy lump to my throat. Beneath the drawing, the artist had written this:

PELEIDES BLUE MORPHO
Kingdom: Animalia
Phylum: Arthropoda
Class: Insecta
Order: Lepidoptera
Family: Nymphalidae
Genus: Morpho
Species: M. peleides

Dear Gloria,

I gathered this information with the help of Wikipedia, so don't tell X, okay? The Blue Morpho is a native of South America. I'm not sure how they got here in such numbers, but get this: The entire life span of the Blue Morpho is only 115 days. 115 days! Carpe diem, Blue Morpho. Carpe diem, Gloria Bishop.

Your friend and amateur lepidopterist,
Calvin Little

Calvin Little, Lepidopterist! Calvin Little, he of the Still Waters Running Deep all over the place. Sweet, belt-wearing, Latin-spouting Calvin, to whom I owed three dollars and seventy-five cents. He had called himself my friend, and for some reason that knocked me out more than if he had professed his undying love for me. *Friend,* as in the noun-not-the-verb, as in real-life, flesh-and-blood *friend.* I wanted to cry with appreciation for him. As I glue-sticked the Blue Morpho into the GBBoE, it occurred to me that my mind had snapped a photograph of Calvin—Calvin kneeling in the sunshine, his brilliant hair aflame in the light, cradling that butterfly in his freckled hands—and that I might just carry the image with me for the rest of my life.

6

The View from Underground

EN ROUTE from the shower, resplendent in glasses and towel turban, I thought I heard the phone ringing in room 317. As I took off running, flip-flops smacking obscenely on the floor, I imagined I looked like some sort of demented diva-duck.

I hadn't yet gotten used to communal living and prayed nobody would see me wearing flip-flops, which I refuse to condone as actual footwear outside of the necessity for maintaining proper dorm hygiene.

"Hello?" I gasped into the phone.

"Gloria? It's Chloe. Are you up?"

"It appears that I'm up."

"Listen, I think I've got it. I think I know where the next clue is."

"That's awesome!" I shrieked. "Where?"

"I think we should all go together. Can you meet at the Egg Drop in half an hour?"

A little guiltily, I thought of Jessica's note and its implication that I should join her for breakfast. Oh, well. She wouldn't mind. "Yep. Half an hour."

"Fabulous. I just talked to Calvin, but Mason's phone just keeps ringing. I need to dry my hair. Will you try to call him again for me? It's extension twenty-nine."

"Well, I—"

"Okay, great. See you in a bit!"

The dial tone buzzed accusingly in my ear. *Chloe*, I thought, *you suck*. I punched in the numbers for Mason's room but hung up before it started ringing. Deep breath. Okay. One more try. I let it ring at least nine times and was about to hang up again when this baritone doomsday voice answered.

"You've reached the Decline of the West; this is Edward Softly speaking."

"What? Mason?"

"One moment, if you will."

I heard a shuffling sound, followed by mumbling sounds, followed by Mason's actual voice, sodden with sleep. "Hmmmo?"

"Mason?"

"Hmm?"

"It's Gloria. Listen, you need to get up. Chloe thinks she knows where X's next clue is and she wants us to meet at the Egg Drop in like thirty minutes. Okay?"

More shuffling, a noisy yawn. "Wait a minute. You're talking too fast. Now, what?"

I sighed and repeated myself, alarmed to discover that my heart was beginning to bonk around obnoxiously in my chest. "Will you just get up and meet us there as soon as you can?"

"Well, wait a minute. Slow down a minute. What'd she say? Where's the clue?"

"I don't *know* yet. Chloe has organized this powwow and asked me to call you. I'm only calling because she asked." I felt it was important to make that much clear.

"What's Calvin say?"

"I don't know. I mean, he doesn't know yet, either. He's meeting us there. So hurry, okay?" God, I couldn't wait to hang up.

"Wait a minute."

"*What?*"

"What are you all worked up about?"

"Nothing. I'm not worked up. Who the hell is Edward Softly?"

Mason groaned. "My roommate," he said. "He's so obsessed with H. P. Lovecraft that I think he actually thinks he's H. P. Lovecraft. He also thinks it's approximately 1922."

"Perfect." I laughed. "H. P. Lovecraft and the Mad Hatter. Are yall running a freak show over there or what? Fun-house rides and warped mirrors, the whole shebang?"

"Wanna come over and be the Bearded Lady?" Mason quipped, not missing a beat.

"Um, pretty sure I don't have a beard," I said. A nonsensical response to a nonsensical dig, but still my hand rose reflexively to my chin, just to make sure. I gathered my robe more tightly around me and shook my hair free of its towel turban, once again paranoid that Mason with his demon gaze could somehow see me sitting there in my diva-duck getup.

"We're also auditioning for the spangle-clad aerialist, but you'll have to get in line." I could hear his smug grin through the phone.

"I am hanging up now, Mason. Half an hour, okay?"

"Okay."

Without saying bye I returned the six-ton receiver to its cradle and vowed that I would henceforth keep one-on-one communication with the Mad Hatter to an absolute minimum because, good God, the boy made my *teeth* hurt.

On the way to the Egg Drop, I spotted Calvin, his bright head lowered in thought, crossing the street in his trademark bashful lope. "Hey!" I yelled, waving mania-cally. "Calvin, wait!"

Calvin offered a gallant elbow and I linked my arm with his as we crossed the street. "Hey, thanks for the butterfly. You're quite an artist."

"You're welcome," Calvin said. "It's just scribbling, really. Just something I like to do on the side."

"Oh, on the side," I teased him. "You know, when I'm not working out algorithms and playing around with Punnett squares and whatnot."

Calvin grinned sheepishly and opened the door of the Egg Drop for me. Chloe was already there, hunched over the jukebox. When she saw us come in, she beamed and waved her arm in the direction of the table we had occupied the day before. "I ordered us some pancakes and coffee," she said. "Breakfast is on me today. Be right there. I'm trying to get this thing to play my song."

I slid into our booth and Calvin followed. I watched with interest as he carefully unwrapped his napkin-rolled utensils, placing his fork, knife, spoon, and chopsticks in perfect, proper alignment with the space that would soon be occupied by his plate. GoGo would have wept.

Chloe crooned along with the jukebox—some song in inscrutable French—as she waltzed toward the table, one hand pressed to her chest in a dra-matic swoon of emotion. "Oh, God, yall, I love this song," she gushed, spilling herself into the booth.

"Can you imagine being gorgeous, *and* being a singer-songwriter, *and* having your songs all over movie sound tracks and jukeboxes in America, all while being the First Lady of France? It's wild. It's ridiculous and unfair. Why am I not French? Why?"

Calvin and I watched patiently as Chloe closed her eyes and sang in perfect French along with the jukebox, pausing during the instrumental parts to take a long invisible drag from a chopstick. When our pancakes and coffee arrived, she looked up at our server — same one from yesterday, I wondered if she ran the place entirely by herself — and gushed, "Oh, Xiu Li, I am in the wrong century. I am in the wrong *country*. These pancakes are beautiful! *Merci*."

"This country not so bad," Chloe's new best friend Xiu Li replied. "Enjoy, enjoy, enjoy." She was talking about the pancakes but it seemed like she was talking — with no small amount of gratitude and enthusiasm — about the world itself.

"May I have a glass of milk, please?" Calvin asked Xiu Li, who grinned, nodded, and disappeared with a friendly hum on her lips. I liked Xiu Li. She seemed to be the sort of person who could kick your ass very, very gently.

Chloe and I exchanged an amused glance at Calvin's milk, and then the jangly bell on the door heralded the arrival of the Mad Hatter, who had clearly woken up that morning in rare form. I mean he obviously knew we were there, right? But he walked in and acted all blasé, checking out the display of free newspapers in the entryway, *La la la, I have all day, the world revolves around me, la la, and oh! Who's this lovely girl spinning on a bar stool at the breakfast counter?*

"Mason's here," I deadpanned. "Taking his sweet time as usual. He's talking to some girl over there."

Chloe turned around to look. "I don't know about those shoes. A little stripper-ish for nine in the morning on a Tuesday. Do you think that's his girlfriend?"

"Okay, yall should really not be staring like that," Calvin said. "Pass the syrup, please."

Chloe rolled her eyes and feigned oppression. "Calvin, please. You and your milk. Why shouldn't I stare? Seems like it's always *us* waiting for *him*. Have you noticed the pattern?"

"Yes," I answered, trying to concentrate on my pancakes. They really were delicious. Xiu Li was my hero.

"Good morning, good morning," Mason intoned brightly as he folded himself into the booth beside Chloe. "Are these for me?" He nodded at the pancakes.

"Yes, Your Highness," Chloe said. "Courtesy of *moi*. Who's the girl?"

"Her name's Andrea," Mason answered, carefully avoiding everybody's eyes.

"Andrea," Chloe repeated, balancing a bite of pancake between her chopsticks. "Right, right. Should I ask her to join us, or what?"

"Nah. She's a friend of my sister's. Just some girl."

"You have a sister?" Calvin inquired, as if this were a revolutionary piece of information.

"Two sisters, actually. The female-to-male ratio in my house is three-to-one, four if you count the dog."

Three females, one male, a watchdog. It was time to change the subject. "That's fascinating," I broke in, "and Mason, I'd love to know more about your family tree and your pseudo-girlfriend at the counter over there, but let's get on with it, shall we? Chloe. Tell us what you know."

Chloe nodded and leaned in close to us, her green eyes bright with mischief. "Right," she said. "So I think the clue's waiting for us in the tomb of Thomas McGrath."

Urn, as in Grecian Urn, as in the Urn in Which the Remains of Thomas McGrath Are Buried in a Crypt Beneath Morlan College's Notoriously Haunted McGrath Hall. Call it a stretch, but still: Once Chloe suggested it, the total and complete obviousness of it felt like a blow. Had it really taken us eighteen whole hours to figure that out? I scowled and huffed all the way to McGrath Hall, where we were met at the welcome desk by a sunny creature whose name tag said MEGHAN.

"Good morning, welcome to Morlan College, can I help—" Meghan chirped, rising from her seat, but as soon as she saw Mason, her voice flattened and dropped a couple of octaves. "Oh. Hi. What are you doing here?"

Mason sauntered past the rest of us and plucked a card from the little card holder on Meghan's desk. "Administrative Assistant," Mason read aloud, nodding his head in exaggerated approval. "Sounds important."

Meghan crossed her arms over her impressive chest and closed her eyes for longer than a blink. "Mason, I'm working. One more time: Can I help you?"

"Actually," Mason swaggered, "my friends and I were hoping for a look at McGrath's tomb."

"There's a campus tour at eleven," Meghan replied, eyes averted. "Come back then." Having provided her final answer, she sat back down and busied herself with a stack of papers on the desk. Mason regarded us with an oh-well shrug that was, hello, just not going to fly with me, not at all. We were on a *mission*.

"Meghan," I said, approaching the desk in my best imitation of bravado. "Hi. My name's Gloria and these are my friends Chloe and Calvin. The Mad Hatter here is just along for the ride."

"Right," Chloe offered, catching on. "He's our resident Necessary Evil—don't pay any attention to him at all." This earned Chloe a stunned gape from Mason and sent Calvin shuffling red-faced to a nearby bench, where he sat down and pretended not to know us.

"So Meghan," I continued. "We're Geek Campers, see, and we really, really need to get inside that tomb. Seriously, like five minutes. In and out. Just for a sec."

"It's for a project," Chloe added. "Our teacher's got us on a scavenger hunt."

When Chloe said it out loud, I realized how lame it sounded. Could we be any more ridiculous? I was sure that Meghan, with her shiny hair and shiny business cards, thought we were idiots. I was surprised when she rummaged in her desk and produced a silver loop loaded with keys. "Five minutes," she said, narrowing her eyes at Mason. "Got it?"

Mason grinned as if the triumph were his, and we followed Meghan down a flight of stairs and one long, innocuous hallway, at the end of which was a completely innocuous standard-issue door that could've easily opened to a chemistry lab or a conference room. The door looked like all the other doors, which is to say that, judging by that door, the famous tomb of Thomas McGrath was turning out to be a total buzzkill, not at all like the dank, terrifying morgue I had conjured in my head.

As Meghan inserted key after key to no avail, she launched into tour-guide mode, telling us how every Halloween, five Morlan students were selected by lottery to spend the night locked in McGrath's tomb. It was a very big deal, this annual campus tradition, and students who submitted their names to the lottery became the stuff of legend. "Except if you're this guy Dougie Landon," she added. "A friend of my cousin's roommate? One year Dougie was one of the McGrath Five, and he got so scared that he screamed and pounded on the door for three hours until somebody relented and let him out. Rumor has it he peed in his pants."

"Is that right?" Mason smirked.

"That's how the story goes," Meghan replied coolly. "Ah. Finally." With some effort, she shouldered the door open, and we were met by a decidedly unfriendly blast of cold air. So far I couldn't see anything much, but the darkness and the cold and the whiff of damp from within—that was much more like it. I could feel the fear prickling up along my spine, thrilling and delicious.

"There's a light switch in here somewhere," Meghan mumbled, feeling along the wall. Even with the light on, the space was dim and shadowy. "Enter at your own risk."

Chloe went in first, hopping down four stone steps into a space just big enough for two twin beds, only there were no beds down there, just two rectangular stone blocks, each one roughly the size of an outstretched human.

"That's him on the left," Meghan told Chloe from her station at the door.

"So who's this, then?" Chloe climbed atop the other stone, stretched out on her back, and folded her hands behind her head.

"That's some other random guy; I forget who."

"Chloe?" Calvin asked, peering in over Meghan's shoulder. "Is X's letter down there, or what?"

"Oh yeah," Chloe said. "Lemme look." She swung her

legs over the side of Sir Random's eternal resting spot as if she were lazing about on a sofa. We watched her slide her hands along the walls and climb over McGrath's block, where she crouched on the far side and emerged, triumphant, with an envelope in her hand. "Voilà, *mes amis*! Now, get down here so we can open this thing."

"Why don't you bring it up here, where the light's better?" Calvin suggested.

"Yeah," Mason said. "Bring it up here, Chloe." His voice sounded bored, but his eyes were flicking around nervously.

"No way!" I protested. I wasn't about to miss my chance to explore McGrath's tomb. I took the stone steps two at a time and joined Chloe in the cool of the room. Calvin followed with a resigned sigh.

"I have to get back to the desk," Meghan announced. "In or out, Mason. Either way, you now have" — she checked her watch — "three and a half minutes to get your kicks. I'm not gonna babysit you all day."

As if accepting a dare, Mason leaped all four steps and landed grandly in the center of the tomb. Arms outstretched, he spun around and glared at Meghan. "Happy now?" he asked.

"Almost," Meghan said, and before she shut the door, locking it with an ominous click, she cocked her head at Mason, raised a sly eyebrow, and winked. "Nice hat."

"Fabulous," Chloe announced. "Just fabulous. Mason, do you know every single person in this town?"

"I went out with her freshman *year*," Mason balked, as if anything that happened back in the dark ages shouldn't be held against him. "And it was only because she was a junior and had a license."

Calvin began a calm scan of the room, running his fingers along the walls, where brave legions of McGrath Fives had left makeshift cave art: RUTH '85; ALL HALLOWS' EVE 1993; I AM HUNGRY; THOMAS MCGRATH IS A PUSSY. It was entertaining reading, and added to the thrill I felt at getting trapped in a room with a ghost. It was like I had known from the second she produced that loop of keys that Meghan the Administrative Assistant was going to lock us in. It was almost like I was secretly *willing* her to do it. In my mind I forgave her for going out with Mason and applauded her bold move.

"Hey, Gloria. Look at this." Calvin pointed to an elaborate chalk drawing of a girl with flowing hair and a smile with a secret in it. In an eerie sort of way, she looked like me. "Do you come here often?"

"You know what they say—everyone's got a doppelgänger somewhere." The more I stared at the chalk girl, the more she seemed like an image staring back at me from a mirror. Wild.

"Yeah, well, I hope my doppelgänger is out somewhere enjoying some fresh air, lucky bastard," came

Mason's muffled voice. He was sitting on the floor with his head sandwiched between his knees. "I can't breathe."

"Nobody panic," Chloe commanded. "I've got a ton of supplies." From the depths of her bag she produced a handful of fortune cookies. "Hungry?"

Mason groaned. "Get me out of here. I'm serious."

Calvin the Unflappable reminded all of us that Meghan had mentioned something about a tour at eleven, which meant that our stay in Chez McGrath would be brief. This was buzzkill news to me, but Mason relaxed visibly and launched into that inevitable morbid discussion that everyone seems to have at some point or another—the great debate about What's the Worst Way to Die.

"Man, buried alive. No question. Or stuck in an elevator while everyone sucks up all the air!" Mason shuddered and stuck his head back between his knees. "Can't handle it, man."

Chloe shook her head. "No way. Drowning's way worse than that. Way."

"I'm not into stampedes," I offered. "Did you hear about those people who died at Wal-Mart when the store opened on Black Friday? God, what a way to go out—trampled underneath a bunch of freaks in pursuit of a Wii."

"Yes!" Calvin chimed in. "That was in New York, right? Couple of years ago? And my aunt was actually at that Who concert in Cincinnati when the same thing happened. December third, 1979."

After a pause during which I was (a) almost paralyzed by my vivid imagining of being trampled to death at a rock concert and (b) completely mindfreaked by Calvin's encyclopedic recollection of such horrors, Calvin went on. "That's not the worst, though. The worst is dying in some scenario where you have absolutely zero control. Airplanes. Helicopters. They're the worst. You couldn't pay me to get on an airplane."

"Calvin," Chloe said, squinting with appreciation. "You have categorical knowledge of the absolute weirdest shit. I bet right now you could give me at least four more famous examples of death by smooshing. Go."

Calvin blushed. "It's called *'crowd crush,'* actually. You'd think that people would die from the trampling, right? But really it's asphyxiation."

"Asphyxiation, as in what's happening to me right now while yall're just standing around chatting," Mason complained from his station on the floor.

Chloe ignored him. "Seriously, Calvin. Death by smooshing. Gimme what you got."

"Okay, it's not exactly categorical recall, but there was that Pearl Jam concert in Denmark where a bunch of people got crushed. Can we talk about something else?"

"No, this is fascinating," Chloe said. "Now. When,

exactly, did these Danish Pearl Jam fans get smooshed to death?"

"I don't remember. Can we open that letter?"

"*Cal*-vin."

Calvin sighed. "June thirtieth, 2000."

"I knew it!" Chloe shrieked. "Oh my God, Calvin, you have a photographic memory, don't you?"

"Okay, okay. Look, I do not have a photographic memory. Sometimes my mind hangs on to dates, that's all. I know the Who concert because it happened on my aunt's birthday—my aunt who was there—and I know about the Pearl Jam in Denmark thing because it happened on my birthday. Okay? Where's X's letter?" Calvin gave Chloe a pleading look and held out his hand for the envelope. "Can I see it? Please?"

Chloe gave Calvin another long, appraising look and tipped the envelope into his hand. "Okay, but I'm onto you, Mr. Little."

Before Calvin opened the envelope, he checked to make sure Mason hadn't asphyxiated yet. "Can you hear me? Are you ready?" Mason bobbed his lowered head, so Calvin cleared his throat and read aloud: "Wait here."

I frowned. "What?"

"Wait here," Calvin repeated. "That's what it says."

Chloe and I peered over Calvin's shoulder for confirmation. *Wait here*? Are you kidding? Weren't we supposed to have solved this part of the puzzle yesterday? We could be waiting for the rest of our lives. We could just be hanging out underground with some dead botanist for the rest of our freaking lives! Suddenly I wanted nothing more to do with X. I was so over X it wasn't even funny.

"Well. X sucks," I said.

"I'm hurt," Mason replied, lifting his face from his knees. He looked bleary, drained of his usual electricity. "I'm really hurt that you would talk about me that way."

Cartoon-style, two more heads turned in unison to stare at him. There we were again: Mason Atkinson's three-member Rapt Audience. Nobody said a word.

"You mean you haven't figured it out yet?" Mason grinned. Still there was silence. I felt sucker punched, afraid that if I opened my mouth I would throw up.

"Nice," Chloe muttered between set teeth. "Real nice." In the dim, her eyes glistened.

"Yep," Mason said, rising from the floor and dusting himself off. "I'm the teacher. Second-year English lit major here at Morlan. I picked up this Geek Camp gig for extra cash. You, my friends, are the extra cash." Mason winked at us and waited. The room tunneled into silence, thick and accusatory.

"You're not a teacher," Chloe said, icy cool. "You're a liar."

Once again, Mason—or whoever he was—scanned our faces for signs of life. I stole a glance at Calvin, who was watching Mason carefully, his face arranged in an expression of benign amusement. I lowered my eyes, afraid that my own face would betray the betrayal I felt, the sick feeling at having actually allowed the Mad Hatter to appear behind my eyes before I fell asleep the night before. Willing myself not to scream, I turned to study the cave-writing on the wall behind me: RAGE, RAGE AGAINST THE DYING OF THE LIGHT. Good God, was the whole entire world just crawling with self-absorbed English majors exploiting Dylan Thomas? I hated them all. I wanted out. Out out out out out.

"Kidding," Mason said, breaking into a self-conscious guffaw. His laugh bounced off the walls as the air in the room rearranged itself. "I'm kidding, okay? Of course I'm not X. I'm not a liar, I'm an actor."

"Same thing," Chloe ranted. "You're also an asshole." Clawing violently through her bag, she came up with a cigarette and actually lit it this time. "I don't care how claustrophobic you are," she said on the exhale. "I'm going to sit here and smoke in your claustrophobic face."

"Chloe," I said, "put that out." It seemed important that Mason Atkinson not be *completely* in control of everybody's emotions and behavior.

"Fine, fine." Chloe stomped over to Mason and snatched the top hat from his head. "Have I mentioned that I hate this stupid hat?" She tossed it to the floor, flicked the cigarette on top, and ground them both into a charred mess beneath her boot.

Mason seemed only slightly subdued. "Are you done?"

"Yes," Chloe conceded. "Conflict is not my forte. Just give me—give us—an apology and then we're done."

"I'm sorry, but—"

"No, uh-uuh." Chloe shook her head. "It's not an apology if there's a 'but' in it. Try again."

"I'm sorry. Calvin, Gloria, Chloe, I'm sorry. There. Okay?"

"I didn't think you were X," Calvin said, just so we'd know.

"I'm glad you're not X," I said, which was the truth.

"God, get me out of here," Chloe moaned, and, as if on cue, the door opened in a great *whoosh* of suction and light. I was not at all prepared for what came bounding down the stone steps: a puppy. A puppy! It yipped itself into a blur of brown and white as it spun in circles, chasing its own leash.

"Holyfield!" came a voice. "Holyfield, get back up here!"

The owner of the voice appeared next: a guy with a beard and glasses, wearing what appeared to be a *baby* in one of those contraptions on his chest. A puppy? A baby? I thought life on a college campus was supposed to guarantee the absence of such things. I've never been a huge fan of dogs—all that slobbery loyalty, the basis for which is nothing. Babies? Don't even get me started.

The bearded guy was out of breath. "Sorry I'm late,"

he wheezed—I detected asthma and vague cluelessness, a recipe for dorkdom—"but I'm not as late as you are, right? Holyfield, get down." He adjusted his glasses and stuck out his hand to Calvin, who, of the four of us, must have appeared the friendliest. "Wesley Xavier," he grinned. "And this"—he indicated the vapid passenger on his chest—"is Juliet. You've already met Holyfield."

At the sound of his name, Holyfield—who had revealed himself to be a boxer puppy, and irresistibly cute—perked up his ears. They were floppy ears, not the pointy kind I'd seen on boxers before. One of them, the right, looked a little mangled, a flaw that only added to his appeal.

"Runt of the litter," Wesley Xavier said. "One of his brothers got his ear there, poor guy. My wife's the one who came up with Holyfield."

Weston A. Xavier. Wesley Xavier. Just a simple little switch and suddenly you're a fascinating enigma. Why hadn't I thought of that myself?

"So here we are," X said. "I hope I've given yall ample time to get to know each other on your own terms." He looked around the tomb and beamed. Maybe it was just me, or maybe it was Chloe's recently extinguished cigarette, but as X raised both his arms in a goofy gesture of triumph, I swear I thought I caught a whiff of pot. "Welcome to Secrets of the Written Word."

7

Officer Buckle and the Gloria Record

24 June

Dear Carol,

Girl. I'm writing you from the laundry room in the basement of the dorm and it's about 4,000 degrees in here so I hope I don't sweat all over the page. How's New York? I want to hear all about it. So far Geek Camp is good. X isn't a perv but I think he might be stoned about 99% of the time. Also he's one of those completely dorky guys with a really hot wife. How does that happen? Anyway the wife's name is

Kathryn and she showed up today (we were in a tomb with a couple of dead guys, more on that later) to pick up their dog and their baby, whose name is Juliet and who has our same birthday!!! My new friend Calvin says that statistically speaking if you walk into a room full of 20 people at least 2 of them are more than likely to share a birthday, but still I think it's cool even if the baby just sits around and drools or whatever. The dog is cuter than the baby which I know is a mean thing to say but I can't help it. They carry her around in one of those strap-on things (the kid, not the dog).

Anyway, this afternoon there was a camp-wide field trip and they dragged us to a horse farm where we actually got to watch the actual BREEDING PROCESS. I know, right? Gross but fascinating in a train wreck sort of way. Anyway the farm was beautiful and the trip out there looked like a postcard of Kentucky, all these white fences and rolling hills and whatnot. It was like I knew exactly where I was, you know? Our Louisville is great but there's nothing really Kentucky about it. A week ago I would have told you that's a GOOD thing but now I'm not so sure. My roommate Jessica lives in the actual mountains. At first I thought I'd hate her but she's actually great. Then there's Sonya, who is from Muhlenberg County, like the song. I hadn't heard the

song until she played it for me and it made me realize
what I was missing, just like it makes me wonder
that Kentucky has 120 (!!!) counties and I've spent
my entire life in exactly ONE of them. There should
be some kind of law against bitching about the place
you're from until you've actually SEEN some of it.

Okay it really is so hot in here that I can't breathe
and the bottom of the page is looming so this is it for
now. There's a boy here. It's like I hate him so much I
almost like him. I would not admit this to anyone but
you. No diagnosis yet, please.

I miss you and love you and wish we could go get
a Blizzard. Write me soon, okay?

Love,
Glo

So the laundry room in the basement of Reynolds Hall quickly became my Thinking and Letter-Writing Place. I liked it down there—most of the time it was hot as hell, but aside from the excellent white noise of the HVAC unit and the washers and dryers, it was quiet and cavernous and largely unoccupied. In addition to an ancient TV with actual bunny ears that tuned to exactly one channel (sort of), it also featured a purple plastic CD player with a cracked but functional lid. My first pang of missing my laptop came with the realization that I wouldn't be able to immediately transfer the songs from Alex's CD onto

Indigo, so discovering the CD player was an excellent lark. Alex's CD? Be still, my beating heart. I tried to see how long I could make myself wait to open the package and I held out for roughly twelve hours, which is not bad if you're me. Totally worth the wait: a collection of sixteen songs, eight with my name in the title (in chronological order and spanning four decades!) and eight by some band I'd never heard of and quickly fell in love with called the Gloria Record. Inside, a note:

Dear G-L-O-R-I-A,

Maybe you're not entirely out of my system after all. At the last minute I decided to accept my uncle's summer job offer so I'm leaving Thurs. to help out at his roadhouse in Talkeetna. I'll be there until Aug., then it's on to Anchorage and UAA and the wild beyond, which would be cooler if you were in it. Hope you like the songs. Take care and have fun at Geek Camp.

Love,
Alex

P.S. The U2 song is my favorite live version and it is EPIC!!

If I loved Alex before, I loved him ten times more now that he was no longer in the Lower Forty-Eight. Completely backasswards, but also completely true. His absence, the distance, the mysterious business of a *roadhouse* (I imagined a log cabin, taxidermy, bizarre people drinking absinthe in some seedy saloon) in a town whose name I couldn't pronounce—it was thoroughly enchanting, every bit of it. He wouldn't be back until Thanksgiving—ah, the beautiful, aching *agony* of it! My life was taking on the soft glow of a movie; now this was the kind of romance I was destined for: the kind where you don't have to actually show up with frizzy hair. After all, my handwriting is so much more appealing than my face. If you could have looked inside my head, here's what you would have seen: *Love Alex Love Alex Love Alex Love Alex Love Alex.* What a lovely refrain. I listened to the songs over and over, mining them for hidden meaning.

The lyrics paraded around in my head all night and into Wednesday, which turned out to be Community Service Day. Assignments were distributed by dorm floor, and Reynolds 3 was handed the unfortunate task of entertaining a bunch of three-year-olds at a local day-care center. Suck! Chloe and the rest of Reynolds 2 got to clean up a highway, which sounded marvelous in comparison. Calvin and Mason were in charge of helping local farmers get their stuff ready for market—thrilling! I would have eagerly volunteered to clean bus station toilets if it meant I could escape the torturous sentence that was Dealing with Kids.

Anyway. That's how I came to be standing in front of a little girl named Brayden, whose mouth was still ringed with a violent shade of green from the Popsicle she'd had for a snack. We were on this playground behind the preschool. Brayden was on a swing, and I was standing behind her, contemplating the best way to give her an effective push. I reached out and put my hands on her back, which seemed impossibly tiny—a delicate architecture of bird bones fluttering beneath my fingers. I was scared to death.

"No, yank back real hard on the chains, up here," Brayden ordered, slapping the metal links with gusto. Nothing delicate about her. "Give a big push, like Daddy!"

Like any good lemming, I followed orders. I yanked the chains back as far as they would go and released Brayden, who sailed forward with a gleeful shriek and then—"Watch this, Miss Gloria!"—leaped from the swing and landed hard on the ground. My mind went straight to the dangerous territory of blood and broken bones, but Brayden rose from the mulch unscathed. She dusted herself off, squinted at me, and, apropos of nothing, asked, "Hey Miss Gloria, do you like pineapple?"

"I do," I answered, and the questions continued, rapid-fire non sequiturs that ranged from tornadoes to velociraptors to the very hot topic of Disney princesses.

"Which one's your favorite?" Brayden wanted to know.

"Ariel?" I guessed.

Brayden frowned. Wrong answer. "Why Ariel?"

God, this was tedious. "Well," I said, "first of all, I can appreciate that Ariel is a rebellious soul."

Brayden squinted.

"She doesn't let anyone tell her what to do, you know? Also, it's cool that she shares a name with a character in a play written by this very famous guy named William Shakespeare. The play's called *The Tempest*. You'd like it."

"*The Tempest*," Brayden repeated. She was the kind of kid whose brain locked on to things, I could tell.

"Yeah. Tempest means storm."

Brayden's eyes got huge. "You mean like a tornado?"

"More like a hurricane," I said.

"Do you know what?" Brayden asked. Too excited to wait for my reply, she answered herself, giggling and spinning in circles: "They don't have tornadoes *in heaven*!"

I didn't know what to say to that, so I followed Brayden's lead and, arms flung out to my sides, started spinning as fast as I could. The world tipped sideways, trees spilling into the sky. Everything was hilarious. Everything was hilarious and sad. I waved across the playground to Sonya, beckoning her to save me from all that dizzy hilariousness. She jogged over and crouched down in front of Brayden, hands on knees.

"Hey there," she said in her normal Sonya voice. Sonya didn't change her voice—or anything else about herself—for anybody. "We're going to play some basketball. Do you want to play or what?"

"I want to play!" Brayden screamed, and she took off running in the direction of a noisy circle of toddlers and a hoop that was about four times too high for them. Jessica was over there sinking one neat basket after the other, and the kids were clapping wildly.

"How are they going to reach?" I asked.

"They don't care if they can reach or not," Sonya said. "Trust me."

"But what about teams? How are we going to do this?"

Sonya planted her hands on her hips. "Girl, weren't you ever three years old?"

I stared at her and blinked. I tried hard to remember being three. The best I could do was four, this time when my mother took me to a baseball game, just the two of us. It was a summer day, like this one. Dusk. My mother is always in a hurry, always in a rush. That night, though, she was still. Peaceful. Absentminded, maybe, because as we sat there, ears tuned to the satisfying crack of ball against bat, my mother gently scratched my arm—just kind of absentmindedly stroked my arm and hummed as she watched the game. Who knows where her mind was drifting. What matters is that she was there, and she was happy, and that baseball will forever be this for me: my mother's touch on my arm.

"Tell you what," Sonya said, grabbing my hand, yanking me back to myself. "How about a do over? For the next twenty minutes, you get to be three again. Watch and learn."

So for the next twenty minutes, I watched Sonya and Jessica as they dazzled the kids with their basketball moves and talked to them in easy, friendly chatter about the star players on the UK basketball team. These kids were *informed*. They knew exactly what was going on. By the time we moved back inside for circle time and a story, my friends had acquired fifteen pint-size devotees. I, who had never babysat a single day or minute in my life, sat back in Deer-in-Headlights mode and watched, awestruck.

Sonya sat cross-legged on the floor, and all the kids made beelines for her lap. "Whoa, whoa, whoa," she said. "I've only got one lap. Miss Jessica has a lap and Miss Gloria has a lap, and the rest of all yall're gonna have to sit down on your bottoms—right now—or I'm not going to read this story. Are we clear?"

It was like musical chairs, only musical laps: Jessica got swarmed. Nobody wanted my lap except for Brayden, who approached me shyly and grinned. "Can I sit with you?"

I patted my crossed shins. "Have a seat."

Brayden lowered herself onto my lap, and Sonya, having successfully quieted her young charges, started reading a book she had chosen for do-over three-year-old me. It was called *Officer Buckle and Gloria,* about a cop and a dog. Gloria was the dog, of course. Brayden and her friends hung on every word. Sonya was the best: theatrical and funny in all the right places, hushed and serious when the story called for it. Brayden's fingernails were lined with dirt, and she wore two ladybug barrettes in her hair, which was a tangled mess but also smelled of sunshine and playground mulch and some other unnameable kid fragrance, and the solid warmth of her little bird body brought me, at one point, dangerously close to tears. I chalked it up to sleep deprivation, but when it was time for us to go and Brayden threw her bird arms around my neck in a mighty strangle-hug, I felt the pinpricks behind my eyes again and knew it was something else.

"See?" Sonya said on the bus home. "You just gotta talk to them like they're people. That's all anybody wants, I don't care how old or young they are."

I smiled. It felt like the truest thing I'd ever heard. "Sonya Henderson, you're my hero."

"You're my hero, too," came Jessica's voice from the seat in front of us, where she had stretched herself out for a nap. "Hey, do you have any gum?"

The bus rumbled on and I pressed my head to the window, watching the farms lilt past, one green swoop and then another, a ribbon of white fences tying them together. Horses grazed and idled, and there were foals too: these tiny baby horses, all wobbly and adorable on their spindly legs, hovering close to their moms and swishing their tails in mom-baby unison. Good God, Brayden had asked a ton of questions. She was a lot like Scout Finch that way. Let me tell you some things I've learned about the Scout Finches of this world. First of all, they show up when you least expect them to. Then, when you least expect it, they go and break your heart into about a million pieces. The other thing—and this is seriously, truly true—is that I've got some kind of built-in *radar* for the Scout Finches. I can spot them from a mile away.

8

The Assignment

"OKAY, SO. So what we're going to do is this. We're going to write our own paragraphs in the style of Fitzgerald. The idea is to ask yourselves, what makes a sentence Fitzgerald-esque? And then write a paragraph or two on your own. Got it?" X regarded the four of us through his wire rims and grinned.

I blinked. Like my friends, I was still trying to reconcile my preconceived notion of X with the actual person now standing before us. In our minds each one of us had conjured a different image of X, but they were all pretty much variations on a theme. The theme, it turned out, was the exact opposite of the reality. I had imagined X as a dark, dangerous envelope-pusher—maybe even a masked vigilante in a cape—not some earnest, mild-mannered new dad who was allergic to ragweed and had spit-up all over the shoulder of a T-shirt bearing the words I WENT TO THE MOUNTAINS BUT THEY WEREN'T THERE.

I got the sense that X could sort of sense our disappointment.

"Why aren't your pencils moving? Time's a-wasting, people."

This new enthusiastic X was quite a departure from the Stoner X of yon; if he was high on anything today, it was sheer *Gatsby*. I was having trouble tuning in, though. The air conditioner in the classroom building was broken, and my thighs were sticking to my seat. The seat was the kind that's actually built into the desk, the better to make you feel like a prisoner stuck in some kind of elaborate torture device.

Calvin raised his hand. "Sir, could you give us an example?"

X deflated visibly. "Calvin, please call me Wesley. And yes, uh, let me see. Okay, here's an example of what I mean by a truly Fitzgerald-esque sentence." He paged through his book and rose from his perch on the desk when he found what he was looking for. " '*A universe of ineffable gaudiness spun itself out in his head while the clock ticked on the wash-stand and the moon soaked with wet light his tangled clothes upon the floor.*' Now. Isn't that something?" X grinned at us again, urging us to love it with abandon. I wanted to rise to the occasion, I did, but man, it was so unbelievably hot.

"What the hell is a wash-stand?" Chloe wanted to know.

"So do you want us to just use three syllables when one is plenty or what?" Mason asked. "Because that's what it sounds like."

"Excuse me, sir?" Calvin said, raising his hand again as he spoke.

I raised my hand, too. "Can I go to the water fountain?"

"Me too," Chloe added. "I feel major dehydration coming on."

X regarded us in silence with an expression that could have been disappointment but might have been remorse. Remorse tinged with anger, laced with exasperation and weariness? The morning was not off to a good start. X took his glasses off and rubbed his eyes in slow, deliberate circles. "Let's start over," he said, taking a breath. "Let's try this again. *The Great Gatsby,* also known as one of the all-time Great American Novels. A piece of immortal literature written by F. Scott Fitzgerald. Raise your hand if"—and here he paused to loop his spectacles back around his ears, but his voice remained steady and calm—"raise your hand if you give one single solitary shit about *The Great Gatsby.*"

The word hung there in the air: *shit*. The silence that followed buzzed around in my ears. I looked over at Calvin, whose hand shot ramrod straight into the air, and at Mason, who, by way of reply, crossed his legs on top of his desk. Chloe leaned back in her chair, narrowed her eyes to green slits, and smoked her pencil.

"Calvin, get your hand out of the air," X said. "One of the advantages of being seventeen years old and almost eligible to vote is that you don't have to wave your hand around every time you wish to speak."

"Sir, I thought you asked us to—"

"I know what I asked, and I got my answer," X said. "From here on out, there's not going to be anymore hand raising in here, and that's not because I'm trying to *ingratiate* myself with you, but because there are exactly five of us in this room, and it seems reasonable that we should be able to carry on a thoughtful dialogue in a halfway-natural sort of fashion."

Chloe raised her hand. X closed his eyes for a second, and I thought he might get mad, but his voice stayed soft, patient. "Yes, Chloe?"

"So if you don't want to ingratiate yourself with us, why'd you say shit? Wasn't the idea there to, you know, bring yourself down to our level? So we can all be best pals?"

"Excuse me, sir, I just want to say that I—" Calvin broke in.

"Calvin. Dude. I'm talking, okay?" Chloe slid her gaze from Calvin to X. "Because I know all about teachers who want to be your best pal, and I was kind of hoping you'd be more interesting than that, X. Scuse me: X, Wesley, Weston, Dr. Xavier, whatever. How about you just pick a name and go with it?" Chloe paused to extract some bits of pencil eraser from her tongue. "I do, by the way."

X looked around, apparently unsure as to whether or not this last part was directed at him. "You do what?"

"I do give a shit about *The Great Gatsby*," Chloe answered. "I give a very big shit, as a matter of fact. I just don't want you or anyone else to ruin it for me, that's all."

X scratched his elbow and examined the floor. He cleared his throat. "Calvin, did you have a question?"

Calvin looked up in alarm. "I'm sorry, sir. I forgot what I was going to say."

X nodded morosely. "That happens, that happens. What about you, Mason? Gloria? Does either of you have anything to add to Chloe's commentary?"

I didn't like the direction this was going, but I felt compelled to say something. I started to raise my hand but then remembered and stuck it back down in my lap. "Well, X—I'm just going to call you X, if that's okay—I just want to say that we had a really great time finding you. You know, the clues and the hunt and all that." I looked at Chloe for confirmation, and she allowed an almost imperceptible nod. Mason lowered his legs and leaned forward on his elbows, listening. "And I'd say that all that stuff you made us read—the Plato and Keats and whatnot—was really good stuff, that we all really, you know, learned something from it." As my voice left my mouth I realized how ineffectual and stupid it sounded. The words were coming out the wrong way. I wasn't saying what I wanted to say at all.

"Well, Gloria always prefers the chase to the catch, so you'll have to take what she's saying with a grain of salt," Mason added, winking at me in his infuriating way, "but what I think she's trying to say, what I think all of us are trying to say, is that this"—Mason indicated the stifling classroom with a flap of his hand—"really sucks in comparison to chasing down Keats by way of a nice greasy meal at the Egg Drop Café. In other words, bro, you had us, and now you're losing us."

X took this in and gave another solemn nod. Then he broke into a low, private laugh and he bowed his head, shaking it slowly back and forth. "Look," he said. "Look. We have four weeks together, and one of them is almost gone. Let's be honest: I'm not going to change your lives in four weeks. I mean, what can I teach you that you don't already know, right? You know everything worth knowing, right?"

We stared at him and waited. Outside, the cicadas were keening their anxious maraca-rattle in the trees. Somewhere a sprinkler spun its noisy, choppy circle

111

across the lawn. Summer sounds. Ordinary sounds you're tempted not to notice until they're gone in the fall and all of a sudden you not only miss them but long for them.

"The truth is, though . . ." X carried on, rubbing at his beard, "the truth is that I think there're all kinds of things you need to learn, stuff that I can teach you if you'll let me. There's a million things I want to say, a million teachable things, but for now I'll give you just one and then we'll get out of here. We'll take this class outside and start over. Does that sound workable? Does that sound like a plan?"

"Yes," Calvin answered for all of us. "Good plan."

"Okay," X nodded. "Here's today's one teachable thing. The thing is this. It's no secret that the purpose of the Commonwealth Summer Program is to lure all of you people into staying in your home state. Not just for college, but for what comes after. Families, jobs, lives. Whatever comes next." X took a breath and eyed each of us in turn. "It's also no secret—I can tell just by looking at each of you, and I can tell because it's a thing I *recognize*—that you can't wait to get out of here. Am I right?"

I looked around. "You mean out of this room?"

"I mean out of this state. This great commonwealth of ours. You can't wait to get out. Right?"

Nobody said anything, so X railed on. "Listen. It might have been half my life ago, but it wasn't that long ago that I was sitting where you are, counting the minutes until I could pack up my van, haul ass out of Kentucky, move to Oregon, and never look back."

The second hand on the big classroom clock lurched forward, a mighty effort. Who hasn't been driven to insanity by the mocking face of an industrial classroom clock? Every single one I've ever gazed upon has operated at the infuriating speed of molten lava. *I have measured out my life with coffee spoons,* says J. Alfred Prufrock. Yeah, well. I've measured out my life through the molten-lava ticks of classroom clocks.

"So did you go?" Chloe asked. "To Oregon?"

"I did go," X answered. "Four unparalleled years of collegiate bliss for which I am still in considerable debt."

Mason shifted in his seat. "And?"

"And eventually I came back," X answered. "Here I am."

"Why'd you come back?" I asked.

"Graduate school," X replied. "Because that was the plan, right? Go to school as long as humanly possible. Go to school forever and ever and never grow up. Peter effing Pan, people."

I swear, the second hand got louder. *Thwack. Thwack.* X was on a roll. The color was high in his cheeks, and he was clearly hitting his stride. "The other thing is this, so listen closely. Listen up. There was a time when I thought I was so brilliant that I couldn't stand the idiotic, waste-of-time conversation of anybody who was less than absolutely brilliant. My friends and I, we sat around writing our brilliant dissertations, and when we weren't holed up somewhere being brilliant, we were enthralling each other with the sound of our own brilliant voices."

X's brilliant voice was getting boring. I cleared my throat a little to give him a hint.

"Anyway. Anyway, do you know where my dissertation is now?"

We waited. Chloe tapped her pencil on the desk in a tattoo of ennui.

"It's stashed up in some dusty fifth-floor archive room in the library of the University of Nowheresville, Kentucky, never to be given a shit about again by me or anyone else, just sitting up there rotting and maybe having brilliant conversations with the other hundreds of brilliant dissertations."

"So what's the moral of this story?" Mason asked, impatient. "I don't think I follow."

"The moral of the story? The moral of the *story* is that once upon a time I wanted the whole world from everyone I met—sun moon stars, give me the whole thing, I want it now, I want it in perfect MLA style. And now? *Now* I know that the best you can ask of people is that they just—I don't know—that they just show *up,* do their part, treat people nicely, pay their taxes. Contribute something halfway decent to society. I'm not necessarily talking about contributing a dissertation, either. I'm talking about pulling your own weight and figuring out what it is you love and then doing it. Not just talking about it or waiting for someone else to do it for you, but actually honest-to-God doing the thing you're meant to do."

I had a feeling that what X was saying had nothing to do with us, or the Secrets of the Written Word, or Geek Camp in general, or anything in that horrible, volcanically hot classroom. I chewed the inside of my cheek, thinking it over. I wished Carol were there to filter through all the soul-searching and help me decipher X's point.

"So what's your point?" I asked, before I could stop myself.

"The point," X repeated. "The *point* is that if I can teach any of you one single thing, it's that it is not your parents' job to take care of you and make you happy and save your sorry asses until you are eighty-five years old. Each one of you is going to walk out of here with a big fat scholarship in your pocket, and if there's anything I can do between now and then to help you figure out that that is a big deal—a big deal not to be taken for granted—then I'm going to do it."

I nodded. A nod with kind of a smirk in it, just in case. "Well, all righty then."

"What's in Oregon?" Mason asked.

X shrugged. "What's in New York? What's in Topeka? What's in France?"

"*Tout le monde,*" Chloe cut in, glowing.

"I'm not coming back," Mason said evenly.

"And that might be what's right for you," X said. "It might be what's right for all of you. But because I get paid the big bucks to convince you that Kentucky is worth your time—not just your time but your future—I'm going to try to do it. I've got a handful of weeks, and that's the plan."

"Ambitious plan, there, X," Chloe said.

X nodded. "And really. Seriously. It's not just because I'm getting paid. It's because I mean it. I mean it when I say that this place is worth it—and if it's not worth taking that scholarship when you graduate, then it's worth coming back later. Your great state needs your minds and your tax dollars, ladies and gentlemen, and I promise you, before you go home next month, I will have provided you with, what, three?—let's say three—reasons to think about staying. Okay?"

Mason smiled. "You're on. I dare you."

"Game on," X said. "Any questions?"

"Yeah," Mason said. "Here's a question. What's all this sanctimonious proselytizing have to do with *Gatsby*?"

X cleared his throat and looked at the ceiling for three excruciating thwacks of the second hand. "Look. A lot of things have changed since my days up in that Ivory Tower, during that grand romance I had with my own superior intellect. I mean, look at me! I am old and fat and have a mortgage and have not slept through the night in approximately three months. On the other hand, I love my wife and I would seriously drive a truck over anyone who ever dared to hurt my kid. I love them so much it makes my stomach hurt. What I'm saying is that my priorities have done one-eighties in ways you wouldn't believe, in ways I never would have guessed if you had asked old Ivory Tower–brilliant me way back in the day. But man, *The Great Gatsby* still tears me up. It tears me up. It still works its magic on me just the way it did when I read it for the first time in ninth grade, Campbell County High School, a hundred years ago. That much hasn't changed, and it's worth something, it is, *it is*."

Calvin extinguished the silence that lingered after this little monologue. "Excuse me, sir?" he asked, frowning at his notes. "Was that one teachable thing or two?"

X gave Calvin a weary smile and spread his arms wide. "It's all the same thing, Calvin. It's all just one big teachable thing."

"So," Calvin said, staring at his hands, "what if I always wanted to stay? What if I never wanted to leave in the first place? What's that say about me? I mean, does that say there's something wrong with me?"

X paused, caught like the rest of us in the spell of Calvin Little. It was something, the way that Calvin's goodness—his remarkable way of just being absolutely nobody else on this earth but himself—could throw a person for a loop. "Maybe," X said, "maybe it says

117

you're wise beyond your years. Wise beyond my years, even."

X zipped the copy of *Gatsby* into his bag and was making for the door when we heard the unmistakable clatter of puppy nails skittering down the hall. Holyfield appeared in the doorway, panting and grinning and trailing a leash with nobody on the other end. A couple seconds later Kathryn, the (visibly exhausted but still stunning) wife, appeared with baby Juliet strapped to her chest. "I'm really sorry," she said to X. "I'm sorry to barge in on you like this, but you're gonna have to take the dog. I can't handle them both." She looked at the four of us and waved, a gesture that seemed to require great effort. "Hi, yall."

"Another teachable moment!" X declared. "It's never a good idea to acquire a newborn puppy immediately after you acquire a newborn person. Word to the wise."

The thought of ever acquiring one, much less both, of those things was enough to send me running headlong into the sea, but Holyfield was cute. I couldn't help it. He trotted over to me and lifted his front paws onto my knee, digging tiny daggerlike puppy claws into my skin. "Ow," I said. "Get down." Holyfield lifted his ears and cocked his head to the side, like, *Really? Are you serious?*

"Oh, good," X said. "Gloria, you be in charge of Holyfield. We're moving outside. I'll meet yall at the Kissing Tree in five."

As it turned out, the romance and lore of Morlan College did not end with the curse of Thomas McGrath. There was also the legend of the Kissing Tree, which, apparently, was the very same ancient sycamore we had swung on and laughed beneath just days before. X told us the story: The tree was more than two hundred years old, and for more than two centuries people had been meeting beneath it to kiss and be kissed. According to campus tradition, a kiss under the Kissing Tree on the night of a full moon was a sign of a union destined to result in marriage.

"Oh please," Chloe said, rolling her eyes. "I cannot believe that we are more than a decade into the new millennium and there are still people buying into that fairy-tale, happily-ever-after, marriage-is-the-end-all crap. Have you seen the divorce statistics lately? Dude, talk to me about marriage when it's legal for everyone." She knocked on the tree. "*Ça va, monsieur arbre?*"

I turned away so Chloe wouldn't see me blushing. I wouldn't have admitted it to anyone, but I liked the story. I liked that the tree had been around so long, and I liked to imagine the sweetness it had borne witness to over so many seasons and years. Surely in all that time there had been storms—there had been lightning and drought and snow and ice and the constant threat of a bulldozer coming to make way for something better—but the tree had outlived them all. I liked to think that the kissing was what kept it alive for so long. I mean, I can believe in a story like that.

"So what we're going to do is this . . ." X was saying. He was sitting on the grass with Holyfield in his lap. The dog, batting at a bee, looked like one of those inspirational posters they sell at elementary school book fairs. I was vaguely aware that X was giving us an assignment, that Chloe and Calvin and Mason were nodding and writing stuff down, but I was still adrift, still hooked on the story of the tree. I walked around the other side of it, running my hands along the ghostly white bark. I wouldn't have been surprised to feel a heartbeat there. I wouldn't have been surprised to find, there in a hollow of the trunk, just above eye level, a pocket watch or a figurine carved out of soap. Just in case, I reached in, hoping. There was nothing there, of course, but there could have been. This tree was Boo Radley's dream.

"Gloria?" came X's voice. "Care to join us?"

I got on the swing and sailed out above their heads. It was a great swing; it really was. It made you feel suspended in midair. It made you believe in the possibility that time could stop and you could be held forever in that butterfly moment just before the roller coaster plummets down the first big hill. "Sorry," I said. "What'd I miss?"

"The Great American Novel," X said. "What's yours?

You have until the end of camp to make us love it with all our hearts. That's your job."

I looked around, still breathless from the swing, not really getting it.

"I'm doing *Gatsby*," Chloe said with a warning glance. "I called it."

I used to think I wanted to be a teacher. I used to think I'd love nothing more than to get up in front of a bunch of impressionable young morons and thrill them with everything I know about Shakespeare, which is kind of a lot. Then I decided I couldn't do it. I couldn't teach something I loved that much—it would be like giving it away, or worse: giving some part of *myself* away. It's selfish and awful and stupid, but there it is. Also, I can't be a teacher. That would interfere with the Plan.

"What'd you find in the tree there, Gloria?" Mason asked, grinning at me. "Spelling-bee medal, maybe?" He was holding something in his hand, and it took me a second to realize it was GoGo's book. *My* book.

"Don't touch that," I said. My voice came out in a raspy whisper; I didn't feel prepared to speak. "Put it back, okay?"

Mason surprised me by returning the book to my pile of stuff on the ground: my bag, the GBBoE, the notebook I had bought expressly for this class, which was so far full of nothing. "Sorry," he said, and he sounded (mostly) genuinely apologetic.

"*To Kill a Mockingbird*! Great choice, Gloria," X said, and even did this ridiculous and embarrassing clap. Holyfield yipped in alarm or approval.

"Class is over, right?" I asked, gathering up my things. "Because I gotta go."

I did this very stagy march across the lawn, this really theatrical show of hurt and anger so everybody would know how hurt and angry I was. I've been in all kinds of plays; I'm good at this shit. Here's the thing, though: In plays and in movies and on TV, the person who storms off usually gets followed by the person who has made her feel hurt or angry. In real life, Mason Atkinson just kept sitting there on the lawn, and his failure to play his part was the most hurtful thing of all.

9

The View from Above

SOMETIMES I try to think back on my favorite days. The days that stand out in my mind as the best ones I've ever had. The thing I've noticed is this: My favorite days don't happen on the days they're supposed to—I mean, don't get me wrong, I've had nice birthdays and decent holidays, but my favorite days have always been ordinary ones. They're those days when you wake up expecting nothing special and by the time you go to bed you've been handed some little piece of magic. That's how it was for me on June 30, an ordinary day when Calvin Little turned seventeen and experienced flight for the first time in his life.

The day started off ordinarily enough: Jessica stepped on X's note on her way out the door. "You've got mail," she yawned, tossing the envelope onto my bed. "If I'm not out of the shower in six hours, come and wake me up."

Field trip today, the note said. *Meet at the Egg Drop at 9. Wear shoes you can walk in.*

When I arrived at the Egg Drop, Chloe was busy decking the place out in full birthday regalia. She and Xiu Li were standing on our favorite table, affixing streamers to an overhead lamp. "Hey, Glo!" she called. "What do you think? Is Calvin gonna freak out or what?"

"Calvin's gonna kill you," I said. I could have hugged her, though, for remembering. She had told Calvin she would remember and she did.

"Well," Chloe said, lowering herself carefully into the booth, "he can thank me later. So where's X taking us? Do you know?"

"No idea," I said. "But I need an omelet. What's the omelet special, Xiu Li?"

"Bluegrass Omelet today." Xiu Li grinned. "Country ham with cheese."

"One of those with an Ale, please," I said.

"You know, Xiu Li," Chloe said, throwing a casual arm around Xiu Li's shoulder, "people from way out in the country call that *old* ham. It's only the city slickers who call it *country* ham. Very important distinction. Take it from a hayseed, okay?"

"A hayseed who practically lives in Cincinnati," I added.

124

"Um, practically Cincinnati by way of Mousie, Kentucky, which is exactly as tiny as it sounds, and where we call it *old* ham, dude, so don't argue with me."

"This girl, she crazy," Xiu Li said, throwing up her arms. Then she turned to me and winked. "You hayseed or city slicker?"

"City slicker, I guess," I said. "But it's not like that's my fault!"

"City slicker has bright eyes this morning. Bright Ox eyes, both you crazy girls."

"How'd you know we were Oxen?" I asked, stunned and impressed and even more in love with Xiu Li, whom I'd pegged as some kind of prophet-seer from the start.

"It's all in the eyes," Xiu Li said, winking again. "Your sneaky Rat friend, he come in now to drink all my Co-Cola. Watch out for Rat!"

According to Xiu Li's paper menus, those born under the sign of the Ox are *Ponderous but impulsive when angry.* Hello, can you say Poster Child? And then there's the Rat, *Charming and quick-witted, but narrow-minded.* Well. That was the Mad Hatter.

Xiu Li disappeared behind the counter just as Mason breezed through the door. He was whistling and wearing a camera on a strap around his neck. It was one of those old-school 35-millimeter jobs, la-la-la, so hipster cool. Before sauntering over to us, Mason paused to photograph the paper peace cranes that Xiu Li had recently hung in the front window. There were hundreds of them, and they spun in rows on long strands of silver string.

"What's up, Ansel Adams?" Chloe said.

"I like to think of myself as more of a Weegee kind of guy," Mason replied in distracted offhand, and there was that pang again: that mixed-up flare of indignation and suppressed appreciation I felt every time Mason revealed that he liked something that I myself happened to like. It had been happening alarmingly often.

"Always at the scene of the crime," I said, because I couldn't—I absolutely could *not*—resist. "Sounds like you. Is that black-and-white film you've got there?"

Mason gave me the briefest, slyest of looks. *But of course.*

I mean, okay. It's not like I have the monopoly on Weegee, any more than I have the monopoly on Boo Radley, but Mason's apparent familiarity with those dear-to-me figures made me feel the same inexcusable, proprietary way I felt when Carol and I went to see the Magnetic Fields in concert. In the weeks and days leading up to the show I was completely on fire with anticipation, but once we got there I ruined it for myself—and for Carol, who says she's never going to a show with me ever again, who actually left me in the parking lot that night—by feeling all this ridiculous *contempt* for the hundreds of jackasses who were there feigning interest in, *laying claim to,* my beloved Magnetic Fields. I mean, nobody else could possibly love them the way I loved them, right? The worst were the posers who came to school the next day actually wearing the Magnetic Fields T-shirts that they had *bought at the show the night before*. I know. I'm an asshole, just like Carol said. An asshole with a thing for Weegee.

"I'm still trying to figure out how this focus ring works," Mason muttered. "Is the light in here weird? Gloria, act natural." Mason pointed the camera at me and adjusted the lens.

"Get that thing away from me." I covered my face with my hands and hauled off to the bathroom. If there's one thing I can't abide, it's cameras. Ever since arriving at Morlan I'd been in a heated debate with Jessica about the camera phone she was forever carrying around and poking in people's faces. She would murder a perfectly good moment just to take a picture of it, I swear. She would take a picture of her breakfast if the spirit moved her, and seriously, the spirit did move her, because she actually said *out loud* one morning that she felt like a thing hadn't really happened if she hadn't taken a picture of it. I ask you: How backasswards is that?

I took a look at myself in the dingy bathroom's cracked mirror, on which someone had magic-markered the words FOR A GOOD TIME CALL IKE. They were the same words, same handwriting, same phone number, I'd seen in public restrooms all over town—in the dorms at Morlan, the convenience store just off campus, the art house theater where Chloe dragged us all to see an ancient Charlie Chaplin movie (which Chloe herself cried through and Calvin slept through and Mason talked through and I thought was completely inscrutable). Ike. Who was Ike? I had to hand it to his nemesis: She was thorough. She had put in a lot of hard work. The phone number had imprinted itself on my brain, and I made a mental note to call it later, just to see what would happen. There was my reflection looking back at me with Ike's phone number tattooed across it. The scrawl across my face gave me a feisty little edge, but behind it I was the same me, the same as always. Not a horrible face, but also not a face I wanted preserved forever on 35-millimeter black-and-white film. Pictures never really do anybody any justice. The photograph of the thing is never as good as the picture you take with your mind. I didn't need a picture of Xiu Li's cranes—they were there in my mind, I had seen them, they were part of me now.

"Girl, I thought you fell in," Chloe announced, barging through the door. "Get out here and eat your old ham. X says we have a lot of driving to do. Wait'll you see our fabulous ride!"

I'm pretty sure Calvin's birthday started out as the worst of his life. After we mortified him with a public celebration at the Egg Drop, X dropped the devastating news that we were going to be taking a helicopter ride later in the day.

Calvin was looking a little peaked as we climbed aboard X's rusty old VW bus—this clunky, hubcapless maroon number that smelled faintly of pot but mostly of dog.

"Chloe, if you sit up front, you have to navigate," X announced. "That's the rule."

"Aye aye, captain."

I slid onto the bench behind the driver's seat and pulled Calvin down next to me to save him from passing out. Holyfield, having immediately zeroed in on Calvin's anxiety, took up residence in his lap. From his station in the way-back, Mason leaned over our seat and took a series of pictures of Holyfield, who seemed—no lie—to be actually grinning for the camera.

"Aren't you out of film yet?" I asked. Then, to Calvin: "Relax. Nobody's going to make you get into that helicopter if you don't want to. I promise."

Calvin was absorbed in petting Holyfield—it made me believe all that talk about how petting a dog can lower your blood pressure. "No, I need to do it," he said. "I need to do that and about a million other things. It'll be good. A milestone. Right?" He looked up at me and grinned. "I mean, it's not like I'll be by myself. I'm braver with all of you around."

I grabbed hold of Calvin's hand and squeezed it. "And we're just nicer people in general when *you're* around."

"Thanks for my birthday party."

"That was all Chloe, dude."

"Hey Chloe," Calvin said, tapping her on the shoulder. "Thanks for my birthday party."

Chloe flipped the sun visor down and grinned at Calvin through the little mirror. "No problem, Cal. You can count on me to be your party planner *and* your navigatrix. X, where's our final destination and what's our ETA?"

The bus was loud. I felt like we were all rumbling along in Scooby-Doo's Mystery Machine. X had to raise his voice so we could hear. "We're going to scenic Perry County, my friends. Everybody's going to get a bird's-eye view of what mountaintop removal looks like in real life."

Mason leaned over the seat, invading my space. "So what does that have to do with the Great American Novel?"

X adjusted the rearview so he could make eye contact with all of us in the back. "Listen up, yall. People can say whatever they want about Kentucky—and they will, they *do*—but by God, people around here can write. Must be something in the water. Anyway the writers are the ones getting all up in arms about the mountaintop-removal thing—and people, these are the writers of the Great American Novels of your generation, not the long-ago god-awful past. I'm talking about right now. Important voices, is what I'm saying."

"Uh-huh," Mason said, squinting through the lens to capture X's face in the mirror. *Click.* "Sounds like maybe *you* have a Great American Novel in the works?"

X grinned. "That's classified information there, pal."

"Classified," Mason repeated. "What about these rolling papers back here? Are they classified, too?"

X bounced a pointed look off the mirror. "Mason, this automobile and its contents are my personal property. Kindly keep your hands to yourself."

"Hey Mason, pass me one of those," Chloe called. She made short order of rolling herself an empty joint and doing an imaginary drag. "Fabulous," she mock-choked, squinting her eyes. She turned to X. "Does Kathryn know you smoke weed in here?"

"Chloe, I do not smoke weed in here. And as it happens, Kathryn would rather perish than set foot in this bus. She thinks it's a death trap—you can't lock the car seat in, some nonsense like that. Never mind that we both spent our early years rolling around loose as marbles in the back of a stay-wag and managed to survive."

"See, Calvin?" Chloe said, waving her air-joint around. "We have a much greater chance of dying in this disgusting old moldy bus than we do in a helicopter. Relax."

Calvin smiled and continued to stroke the ears of the sleeping Holyfield, who in his doze had sprawled half onto my lap. His back feet were stretched out like frog legs behind him; they twitched in dreamy rhythm with the *bump bump* of the bus on the road. I envied the dog's easy trust in people—the fierce way he had attached himself to Calvin, who had warmed so quickly to the role of dog-dad. It wasn't long before Calvin himself had fallen asleep, *zonk,* just like that in an open-mouthed torpor. Soon after that, Chloe was out, too, her shiny dark head lolled against the window.

"So much for my navigatrix," X murmured.

For a while I watched the world zip past. X had some awful music going on the bus's neolithic cassette player, and I longed for Indigo and an underwater dreamworld audiospell. I closed my eyes and tried to conjure Alex behind my eyelids, but it had been getting harder lately to see him there, as if my mind's eye had gotten weighed down beneath the distance between Kentucky and Alaska. I was just starting to picture the curve of his cheekbone when I felt a tap on my shoulder.

"What?"

"Close your eyes again," Mason said. "I want to take your picture."

"No," I said. *"No."*

"Why not?"

"I'm camera shy," I said in sarcasm-ese.

"You've got a great face," Mason said. "You know, a great sort of photographable face. It's different."

I could feel myself blushing all the way to my scalp. *"Different.* That's great. That's really wonderful. Just what every girl wants to hear."

"I didn't mean it like that," Mason said. "Never mind."

I returned my eyes to the window, where my reflection hazed and blurred. Camera Shy doesn't even begin to cut it. It's more like Camera Fear. Camera Rage, Camera Hatred, Camera Suck. A terrible disease to have in the new millennium. Two seconds later, another tap on my shoulder. *"What?"*

"Why are you on the defensive all the time?"

"Why are you on my nerves all the time?"

"I don't think answering a question with a question is Socratic, I think it's shitty."

"Then why don't you talk to someone else?"

Mason managed to leave me alone for almost eight whole seconds before he started talking again. "I saw you, you know, in *All's Well*. Last summer. You were really good."

This information hit me with the force of a blow. I had no response at all, so I just turned around and stared at Mason while the blood slowly drained from my face.

"I said you were good. I remember you. It's a compliment. You know, that thing where you say something nice and then the other person says 'Gee, thanks'?"

Really and truly: I felt like I'd somehow been caught. Caught in a camera flash; caught naked in a bear trap, flailing. "What were you doing in Louisville? Why would anyone not from Louisville go to some stupid Shakespeare in the Park in Louisville?"

"Change of scenery," Mason shrugged. "Research."

"Research?"

"I don't know, I was thinking about auditioning for next summer. Meaning this summer, whatever. Going big-town, you know."

I nodded, not really getting it. Louisville had always felt to me like a very small town; Carol and I had been planning our escape for years.

"Anyway, I decided against it, obviously. The play sucked. You, though — you were good. Memorable."

My head was reeling. So he had seen me there, sweating like crazy in that million-degree corset and those stupid farthingales that weighed about six tons apiece. *Memorable.* The word sparkled in my head like a lit match. "Yeah, well. No more plays for me. I'm officially finished with theater."

As soon as I said it I realized the truth of it: that acting had lost its charm for me, had been losing its charm for a long time; that if I wanted to abide by the Plan, I was going to have to come up with some other good reason to go with Carol to New York. The sudden weird certainty and uncertainty made me feel sort of ill.

"Finished? Why? You're good."

"Exactly. I'm very good at being someone other than who I am. Once I started thinking about that, it struck me as weird. Scary-weird. Besides, the stage, the lights, the applause—that's not what I liked about it." Sleepy Holyfield's leg twitched in my lap; I absorbed myself in petting him so I wouldn't have to look at Mason. This conversation was edging into dangerous, nobody's-business territory.

"So what'd you like about it?"

"I liked telling a story. I liked getting to actually be *in* the story, you know? Making something on the page come alive."

Mason folded his hands behind his head and nodded. "I get that."

"But there was so much about it I didn't like. All that chummy, loud, drama-club bullshit, look at me look at me look at me. And just a second ago, when you said 'All's Well'? God, I hate that, too. Why can't people in a play just say the whole name of the play they're in? I mean, it's never The Pirates of Penzance, it's always, yeah, I got the lead in *Pirates*. I'm working on lights for *Pirates*. Opening night for *Pirates* is in two weeks. Little stuff like that just started getting on my nerves. You know?"

Mason shook his head, suppressing a smile. "You drive a hard bargain, Gloria Bishop."

"Oh, and the way people would say *play practice* instead of *rehearsal*. That drove me insane, too. You're not playing a sport. You're not playing an instrument. It's not practice! I had this idea that if I went to New York, people would call it *rehearsal* and then I'd be satisfied, but I think I'm starting to figure out that nothing about that whole world is really going to satisfy me. It's all just pretend. Just one big ego-fest."

Mason narrowed his eyes but kept smiling. It was interesting, the way his face could convey more than one thing at the same time. "So what you're saying, basically, is that you're a huge snob, you're way better than everyone else, your own ego is too big for the big ego-fest, and that this silly acting business is best left to stupid little plebeian morons like, oh, I don't know, me?"

"That's not what I'm saying!" But it was, I realized. It was exactly what I was saying. It was awful. Already I was wishing I could erase the words and start over. That I could fling myself out of the Mystery Machine and hitchhike back to Morlan ASAP.

"Don't you want to know what *I* like about acting?" Mason asked. He was looking at me through the eye of the camera, adjusting the frame.

"I can't wait to hear." This time I stared at the camera head-on.

"I like how you get to get up inside a character's head. You know, learn how people think and operate." *Click.* "It makes you see people in a different way." *Click.* "Makes you see the world in a different way."

I rolled my eyes, more out of habit than anything else. I was starting to realize that I had almost as many obnoxious habits as Mason. He was my evil doppel-gänger: that's exactly what he was. "That's a gorgeous sentiment, really, but it's not going to change my mind. I've officially, as of this moment, broken up with the stage."

"Ah. The better to spend time with your boyfriend, right?" *Click.*

"Who said anything about a boyfr—" I started, but at that moment I felt something warm seeping through my shorts. "Holyfield!" I screamed. "Oh my God, X, your dog just *peed* on me!"

Holyfield woke up, Calvin woke up, Chloe woke up, X veered the bus onto the shoulder. There was general chaos and racket, and Mason Atkinson, as you might have guessed, was laughing like it was just the funniest thing that had ever happened, ever in the world. Despite all of this horror, or perhaps because of it, there was a split second as we disembarked the Mystery Machine when it struck me that this was it: the exact kind of kooky family tableau I had always longed to find myself in. Finally, finally, I knew what it felt like to be surrounded by siblings on that madcap adventure that is the Proverbial Family Road Trip. If I hadn't been soaked with dog pee, I might've actually cried.

"He hardly ever has accidents anymore, I swear!" X protested. "Gloria, I am so sorry. What can I do?"

"Everybody back up," Chloe ordered, and she drew a wad of Egg Drop napkins out of her bag. "See how important it is to be prepared?" She climbed into the bus and mopped up the pee. Then she dug back into her bag and produced some hand sanitizer, which she applied to a fresh napkin and swiped across the seat. On her third and final rummage into her seemingly bottomless bag, she came up with a tiny black skirt, the kind of thing I'd never wear in this or any other lifetime. "Here, put this on." She tossed the skirt to me and hopped out of the bus. I just stood there, looking around like an idiot. Holyfield cowered at my feet, cocking his head in apology. It was impossible to be mad at him.

"It's okay, buddy," I said, kneeling to scratch behind his ears. "Just don't do it again."

"Get in there and get dressed," Chloe bossed. "We'll wait out here. Just hurry *up,* dude. I'm sweltering."

I had no choice but to climb back inside the Mystery Machine and change into Chloe's skirt. Just to make triple-quadruple sure nobody could see me, I kind of crouched down onto the floor. Their voices were bouncing around out there: Calvin couldn't believe he had fallen asleep, Mason was playing with Holyfield, Chloe and X were discussing the navigational details of the next leg of our trip eastward. Although clearly it was the end of the world, they appeared to have already forgotten about my pee-stained self. I tried to calm myself down, to put it into perspective. I could hear my dad's voice in my head: *Relax, Gloria. Use your head. Try not to make a huge deal out of everything. Resist the urge to make a scene. Resolve to enjoy your life. Don't get into a swivet.* It was the same string of mantras he'd been preaching at me since birth. I've got them recorded in my head for easy access when I can feel myself getting histrionic, when I can feel myself edging into a swivet. *Swivet*: I spent most of my childhood thinking my dad had made that word up. When in ninth grade I encountered it in a book somewhere, I felt all bereft to discover it belonged not just to me but to the world in general. What a buzzkill! Story of my life.

Anyway Chloe's skirt, made for someone Chloe's size, looked ridiculous on me. But it was better than wearing pee, so I tried to shift into Positive Mode as I banged my way out of the bus. "Hey X, did you bring any snacks or anything?"

"What are you, five?" Mason asked. "A snack. Come *on*."

"I have snacks!" Chloe beamed. As we shifted back onto the bus she divvied out the fortune cookies.

"Are we ready?" X asked. "Do we have everybody?" He had this exhausted look on his face, like maybe he was regretting the whole field trip idea.

"Ready," Calvin answered. "I am officially ready to board a helicopter. Let's go."

My fortune was awesome: *You find beauty in ordinary things.*

"I got yours, butterfly man," I told Calvin. "Let's trade."

A friend is a present you give yourself. Also not bad.

"What'd you get?" I asked Mason over my shoulder.

"That's for me to know and you not to know," came the response. "Worry about your own fortune, Gloria Bishop, and I'll worry about mine."

I turned around to shoot Mason a look, and he got me: *Click.* Girl with Fortune, Rolling Eyes.

Perry County, Kentucky, is made of nothing but hills. It's a gorgeous place, the stuff of myth and legend, I'm not kidding. We stopped at a single-pump gas station, and the voice of the guy at the counter was almost hard to decipher, it came out sounding so much more like music than words. We rounded up some Ale-8s, and Link—that was the gas station guy's name—pointed the way, "up yonder a piece, just follow the roadblocks."

And that's what it was like, when you saw it from the ground: a huge, elaborate construction site, only after a while your eyes get used to what they're seeing and you start to piece together that this isn't just the beginning of a coming-soon new strip mall. It's a big cavernous mess where something *millions of years old* used to be, is what it is. Not something you can really put into perspective.

A helicopter and waving pilot stood waiting for us. Walking across the packed dirt and rock felt like walking across graves in a cemetery, or walking on the surface of the moon; that's how weird it is to trudge across a mountain when there's no freaking mountain where the mountain should be. We would have to take turns in the helicopter, so I grabbed Calvin's hand and climbed in before he could change his mind. With his free hand, Calvin waved to X and Mason and Chloe, who, holding Holyfield in her arms, lifted his little paw in a return wave. It was much louder in the helicopter than I imagined it would be, so instead of trying to talk to Calvin, I just squeezed his hand and smiled. He squeezed back, smiled back, and then we were off: tilting and floating away from the ground, that wonderful thrill of flight filling up my lungs.

I closed my eyes and imagined myself held in one of those dreams I have sometimes—my very favorite dreams, where I spread my arms out like wings and fly above the rooftops and bridges of my starlit town. As we hovered above the site, the pilot started talking—he was pointing and telling us something we should've been listening to—but Calvin and I, our palms pressed together in a sweaty grip, our heads craned to see out opposite windows, our ears too full of noise to hear the pilot anyway, were already gone, spellbound. Together we looked down, and I don't know how to describe it, I don't know how to say what I saw, only that it looked *wrong*. It was the definition of wrong, is what it was. For some reason my mind spun back to being six years old, losing a tooth, pressing my tongue to the salty absence in my mouth and marveling that a piece of my body that once-upon-a-time had been there—a fact of me—was suddenly and wholly gone.

The long ride back to Morlan was quiet. Mason took up the role of navigator and Chloe dozed in the way-back. The sun was sinking low in a great wistful swirl of impossible colors, brilliant colors you just can't make up or buy, when Calvin nudged my arm and whispered, "Did you see that farm back there? The one we just passed?"

"Where?" I asked, looking back. "I missed it. Horses?"

"Nope," Calvin said, shaking his head slowly. "A *farm*-farm. Cows. Vegetables. Tobacco, too, used to be." Calvin lowered his eyes and then closed them for a second. When he opened them again I caught something there—a peaceful sort of sorrow that made what X had said seem true: Calvin did seem older and wiser than his newly acquired seventeen years. An Old Soul: That's what GoGo would've called Calvin Little. She had this special radar for Old Souls.

"That's my family's farm," Calvin said. "I guess you could also say it's my future."

10

The View from Below

Glo. *Spent the day apartment-hunting, just for the hell. All the good places are in Brooklyn. Saw this one with a garret-like thing where you can be all Virginia Woolf with a Room of Your Own, Señorita Luddite. I know you're sentimental about graduation (Don't deny it. Denial doesn't become you) but I'm thinking sooner rather than later. This city is crawling with assholes (i.e. people at check-out counters don't bless your heart, etc.) but it's magnificent and breathtaking. Never felt so alive. Anyway there are assholes everywhere you go. If you*

want to act and I want to dance, this is it. This is
where we need to be.

Are you in?
Love,
Carol

P.S. Bless your heart, byotch.

Carol's letter made me feel sort of ill. All along I'd been counting the days until we could move away and start our adventurous artistic lives together, but my shifting attitude toward acting was new—I wasn't used to it and didn't know what to do with it. I hadn't yet revealed to Carol that I was growing nauseated by the whole theater business, and somehow the not-telling her, even though I hadn't fully figured it out, felt like a betrayal.

I tried to pinpoint in my mind the exact moment when I decided to bail on the one thing I've ever been halfway good at. Was it when the Mad Hatter appeared beneath my dorm window in all his theatrical glory? Maybe. Maybe it was that moment in the Mystery Machine when Mason and I had a little chat about *All's Well That Ends Well*. Or maybe the moment happened months before that, when GoGo died. She was the one who had taken me to plays, even from the time I was little. We'd go to Actors Theatre and afterward have grown-up espressos in the brick-walled basement bar, and the whole thing would be magic from beginning to end. GoGo volunteered at the theater and was close personal friends with the actors—she'd sometimes even have them over for Sunday or holiday dinners, the ones who were broke (they were all broke; it was part of their mysterious, tragic allure, as far as I was concerned) and far away from their families. So if it was anybody's fault that I had fallen headlong in love with the stage, it was GoGo's. She was the one who encouraged me, said I was a natural, said I should "honor my gift."

Gift. That's hilarious! I'm not gifted at all. I'm just an ordinary girl who once-upon-a-time loved to go to plays with her gifted grandmother. A girl who loved to take the stage and bow before her gifted, proud grandmother when the curtain came down. After the gifted, proud grandmother was gone, none of it was the same. It wasn't the same at all.

Anyway! God. Who knows when the moment happened? All I know is that I had officially instituted an all-new, no-drama policy that I swore would extend to every area of my life. It lasted about four minutes.

"I am done talking about this! Good night!" Jessica stormed through the door and slammed it behind her. "Hi, Glo."

Sonya breezed in a couple of seconds later, and folded her arms across her chest. "Jessica, we are going to get this shit out of our systems right now."

I was stretched on the bed with GoGo's book. If there's

145

anything I cannot abide, it's conflict. I mean, I concocted plenty of conflict in my head all the time, and I sort of took a perverse delight in all that stupid harmless conflict with the Mad Hatter, but this was different. This was my friends in some kind of actual standoff. "Should I go?" I asked, rising to make a hasty exit.

"No!" They both shouted.

"Stay," Jessica said. "We're done talking."

"We are so not done," Sonya said, but she settled herself on my bed with a magazine as if everything were normal. She even helped herself to an Ale-8.

"Bitch, I did *not* give you permission to drink one of those! Put it back."

A lame little knock at the door. Eager-Beaver Jenny. "Girls, is everything all right in here?"

Jessica and Sonya turned to give Jenny an in-tandem icy stare.

"Everything's fine," I blurted. "They're working on their debate for class. Right, Jess?"

"Right," Jessica answered. "Our *debate*."

"Lights out in fifteen minutes. Sonya, I'll be checking your room to make sure you made it back. In the meantime, keep it down. All righty, ladies?"

"All righty," I grinned, waggling my fingers at her. God, poor Jenny. She had absolutely zero life. I felt bad for her, and nothing's worse than pitying people. Who wants to be pitied? Nobody, that's who. I also felt bad because her role as resident adviser was pretty much null and void, because anytime any of the girls on our floor needed something—whether it was a Band-Aid or some eyeliner or a shoulder to cry on about homesickness, heartache, whatever—they went straight to Sonya. She had taken on the all-purpose role of mom, relationship coach, makeover artist, and general ass-kicker. Sonya's one of those people who came into the world as a self-assured thirty-two-year-old; I could never imagine her in an awkward phase, or with a bad hair day, or without the right answer to whatever needed answering. Seeing her at odds with Jessica was enough to make me feel even more ill than I already felt after reading Carol's letter.

"So they took us to Perryville today, Glo," Jessica informed me. "As in the Battle of Perryville, as in the Civil War?"

"You know, the Civil War," Sonya broke in. "That little dispute that happened a million years ago—"

"Try a hundred and fifty," Jessica muttered. She was cotton-balling her face with makeup remover.

"Whatever. It's over! Let's move on!" Sonya gave a weary laugh.

"Oh, let's move *on*," Jessica groaned. "But first let's make a very big scene in the middle of a restaurant in front of the whole world."

Sonya fell silent, pressing elegant fingers to her eyes. I looked from her to Jessica, who was now busy yanking a brush through her hair in angry strokes.

"What happened?"

"I wouldn't call it a scene," Sonya said. "But it might have involved a minor theft."

"Show her," Jessica said, nodding toward Sonya's bag. "Show her your big prize."

"Fine," Sonya said. "Yall can hang it up in your room for decoration and inspiration. How about that?" Sonya reached into her bag and brought out what I thought at first was some kind of T-shirt—had she raided the battle-field gift shop?—but which revealed itself to be a Confederate flag, filched, as Sonya admitted, from the wall of the famous Perryville Battlefield Canteen, est. 1971.

I couldn't resist offering an appreciative guffaw. "You *stole* that?"

"Of course I did! I'm gonna stick it in the bathroom so we can all wipe our asses with it."

"Okay, okay, who am I?" Jessica snatched the flag, jumped up onto the bed, and stuck out her chest in an impressive impersonation of Sonya, who admittedly did like to let her rack lead the way. She waved the flag around and in her best Sonya voice hollered, "Scuse me, scuse me, yall . . . Am I supposed to think this flag is cute?"

I clapped a hand over my mouth to keep from laughing out loud. Jessica, who was not laughing, hopped off the bed and folded the flag into a neat triangle. "For a lot of people, it's a symbol of heritage," she said, her voice low. "It's a way of remembering people who died, you know? That's all. That's all I'm trying to say. I mean, it doesn't really apply to us, to our generation, is what I'm saying."

I had to replay Jessica's words in my head to make sure I'd heard them right.

"*What?*"

"It applies to me," Sonya said.

Jessica shook her head, a quick erasure. "Forget it. Just forget it. That's not what I meant."

"What *did* you mean?" Sonya asked, eyes glistening. When Jessica didn't answer, she turned to me. "Hey Gloria. You're from Louisville, right?"

God. Here it came. I felt like I'd been apologizing for being the Big City girl from the moment I set foot on campus.

"Yeah," I answered. The tension in the room was awful; I felt all three of us hovering around on the verge of laughter or tears. The scales could've tipped either way.

"Yeah, well. Be grateful that you come from a place that actually has more black people than Wal-Marts. That's all I have to say." Wearily, Sonya picked up GoGo's book. "Great book," she said. "I love this book. Who doesn't love this book? The whoooooooooole world loves this book. Sometimes, though, I think about it, and it's like, you know what? White Man Saves the Day. White Writer Gets a Pulitzer."

Jessica groaned. "God, Sonya! Are you *trying* to pick a fight with everyone?"

"What?" Sonya said. "Can't I say how I feel? Can't anybody say anything true around here?"

My face burned. I felt like apologizing, but I wasn't sure for what. "I've always liked the father-daughter part," I said. "You know, the way Atticus loves Scout, how she and Jem are like his conscience the whole way through." This was true: I had always felt like that was me, that I was Scout, that the book had been written for my eyes only.

"Yeah," Sonya conceded. "They sure-as-shit don't make dads like Atticus Finch anymore."

Yes, they do, I wanted to say but didn't. An uncomfortable silence settled over the room. I wasn't really sure what was happening, but I was determined not to be the first person to speak.

"She's also got a jones for Boo Radley," Jessica muttered, smiling sideways. "Give this girl a surprise delivery in a tree and she's yours for life."

I was relieved to hear Jessica's voice return to its gentle self, and I hoped that this was it, that the storm was over, that we could return to ourselves, cracking up and drinking Ale-8 and alternately envying and making fun of celebrities in magazines.

"So X took us on a flyover today," I said, aiming for a casual change of subject. "You know, over a mountain-top-removal site? You guys, it was the freaking most awful thing I have ever seen in my life. It looked like the end of the world, I swear to God."

Wrong thing to say, wrong thing to say. I felt the reverberating gong of the wrongness as soon as the words escaped my mouth and knew it as soon as Jessica looked at me, hard, disbelieving. "Really?" she asked, eyes narrowing. "You swear to God?"

And to make matters worse, I had just sworn to God. You could *Oh* my God all day long, apparently, but you couldn't *swear* to God. Strike two.

Jessica looked from me to Sonya and back to me. Her face was about nine shades of heartbreak. "*I'm* sorry," she said, "but I must not have gotten the memo! Nobody told me it was Shit All Over Jessica Day. I'm very sorry that I was born white, Sonya. Like that's my fault. Like it's my fault that I happen to have ancestors who fought and died in the Civil War."

"Jess—" I started.

"And you," Jessica said, wheeling around. "What do I need to say to you? That I'm sorry about the mountains? Since I tore them down *myself* and all, with, you know, my bare hands. What are you going to do, Gloria? Move to Perry County? Run for mayor? Save mountains for a living?"

I opened my mouth to speak, but nothing came out.

"Have you ever even been there before today? Could you find it on a map if somebody paid you?"

My face was burning.

"The answer is no," Jessica said. "You wouldn't last three seconds in Eastern Kentucky, Gloria. I'm sorry, but you wouldn't. You have absolutely no freaking idea, so don't march in here with your weird shoes and superior attitude and stupid emo music and liberal big-city *shit* and try to talk to me about something you know nothing about."

Sonya rose to her feet, put a hand on Jessica's shoulder. "Jess. Let's cool off. Let's take a walk. How about we just take a walk?"

Jessica shrugged away. She closed her eyes and addressed us in a voice that was quieter now, calmer, but trembling on the edge of something. "I think," she said, "I think I'll go take a walk by myself, thanks, if that's all right with you two. If I have your freaking permission."

Without looking at us, without even opening her eyes, Jessica turned and walked out of the room. We listened to her footsteps on the stairs.

"Okay," I said to Sonya. I was trying not to cry. I had never had a fight with a friend in my life. It's just something I didn't do. "Okay, what just happened?"

Sonya sighed, rubbed her eyes. "Glo. Girl. Haven't you figured out that Jessica is like a millionth-generation coal kid? You were flying around in her backyard. Her mom? Crazy Diane? Hello, poster woman for the Coal Coalition campaign. Coal is paying for Jessica's sisters to go to Morlan and it'll pay for her to go here when she graduates. That's her life whether she likes it or not."

Oh, God. I wanted to die. "What do you mean, coal kid? Like she comes from a family of actual coal miners? Like people risking their lives every day working at the bottom of a mine?"

Sonya looked at me like I was an idiot, which of course I was. "Gloria. Come on. Do you think the people working in the mine are the same people driving around with Coal Coalition stickers on the backs of their Range Rovers?"

I blinked. *Coal Coalition.* The sticker on Jessica's refrigerator, which hadn't fully registered with me that first day and which I had stared at without seeing every time I went for an Ale. And to think I thought it was a freaking band! The Munch, after all, is plastered with Magnetic Fields stickers, and it's not like I'm advertising my love for math (which, while we're talking about my mental lapses, is another thing I'm incapable of understanding). Now that my mind was rewinding, I could see X's sticker on the Mystery Machine, the one that matched so many others I saw on move-in day: SOL COALITION. As in Solar-Powered Energy, of course. As in Get Your Hands Off My Mountains, You Greedy Bastards. God. How had I missed the connection? It was right there in the song

Sonya had played for me about her beloved Muhlenberg County, the song that was her anthem and her freaking ringtone, which by now I'd heard dozens of times: *I'm sorry my son, but you're too late in asking, Mr. Peabody's coal train has hauled it away.*

I was starting to realize that my own keen Powers of Observation, on which I prided myself beyond reason, were selective and mostly ridiculous. The truth was that I noticed things if I cared about them. If I didn't immediately care or understand, they just filtered right through. Expert Reader of Signs from the Universe, Illiterate Disregarder of Actual Signs About Timely Topics Such as Mountaintop Removal. That was me. I was just like Sophie Allen, who had showed up at school one day wearing a shirt that said DARFUR, which she had bought for six bucks on eBay after watching some YouTube video of Ryan Gosling wearing the same shirt while he made out with Rachel McAdams onstage at the Video Music Awards about a million years ago. Somebody asked Sophie if she knew where Darfur even was, and she was all *What?* Because of course she had zero clue and probably thought Darfur was Ryan Gosling's own personal clothing line, like *Hey Girl, You Look Hot in My Shirt*. Never mind genocide, Sophie Allen. Never mind the rape and plunder of mountains, Gloria Bishop. I really was a walking advertisement for why so many people at Geek Camp seemed suspicious of Louisvillians. Those assholes! They don't say they're from *Jefferson County*. Oh, no. They say they're from *Louisville,* of course. What do they know about old ham? Assholes.

"So they're not *miners,*" I said. "Right?"

Sonya threw an exasperated look at the ceiling. "Does Jessica look like freaking Loretta Lynn to you?"

Loretta Lynn: Hadn't she had done that album with the guy from the White Stripes? Alex listened to that stuff. That much I knew. But at this point I knew better than to share a Sophie-Allen-Meets-Darfur observation like that.

"Shit," Sonya said, rising from the bed. I couldn't tell if she was exhausted with me or just exhausted or both. "Girl, you really are straight outta La-La Land. Blows my freaking mind." She stopped to give me a look that hovered somewhere between affection and pity. "Look, I wouldn't worry about it too much. If I know Jessica, she won't be mad at you, she'll be mad at your teacher for taking yall on that flyover on the government's time and dollar. He better watch it—Crazy Diane'll be over here to rearrange his ass before he knows what's what."

"Oh, God," I breathed into my hands. Now I was worried that X was going to get fired, that it would be all my fault, that I had thrown into motion a domino-string of events that would end very badly, all because I had opened my mouth to say something that I believed to be absolutely true. Truer than true. I mean: Mountains trump Humans. Isn't that obvious? Mother Nature gets the final

155

word, and she's not to be messed with, I don't care who you are. It's a fact as simple and profound as the Golden Rule, and it goes way beyond political discourse and bumper stickers, in my naive, idiotic, big-city-moron opinion.

"Yeah, well," Sonya continued, "you never know who you're gonna piss off. Kevin wants to play ball for UK when he graduates, right? Golden ticket to the NBA? Chance to give the granny who raised him a new knee, a decent place to live, money in her pocket for the first time in her life? But there's that whole thing about the dorm where the players live—the Wildcat Coal Lodge, give my ass a break. Talk about the shit hitting the fan, and all over a name. Coal paid for that place, too, and a whole lot of people aren't happy about it, but what are you gonna do? Skip out on your dream, on every single gift God gave you, because you've got some kind of moral hang-up about a building? Because some hotshot holier-than-thou writer pulls his stuff out of the university archives in protest?"

This was all ringing a bell. Who had told me about it? Calvin. In the Mystery Machine, when he was talking about his family's farm. The hotshot writer was Calvin's own personal hero, the author of the book he wanted to present in X's class as his Great American Novel of choice. You learn a new word, you hear it all the time.

"So," I said to Sonya, "if Kevin's going to be a one-and-done and go straight for the NBA, why does he even care about the University of Nowheresville, Kentucky?" Without thinking about it I had stolen X's phrase. "Why does it even matter?"

Sonya rubbed her eyes. "It always matters to some-body. It matters to me, for example, that everybody's got their undies in a wad about the name of a stupid *dorm*, but nobody seems to care about the name of the great big huge hallowed arena where they actually play ball—where they win the games and retire their jerseys and get their asses kissed to high heaven. It's like: New era, people. Name the place after somebody who didn't miss the integration boat."

"An arena by any other name would still smell like like armpits and nachos," I ventured.

"Nice try," Sonya said, half smiling. "You know what sounds good? The Sonya Henderson Center for Basketball Superiority. I oughta write some kind of petition."

I grinned and curled myself into a ball. It wouldn't surprise me if Sonya made it happen. "So what's Kevin going to do?"

Sonya shrugged. "Says he doesn't know yet, but I know he knows. He's gonna do exactly what he's wanted to do ever since he was old enough to say *Wildcat*, old enough to put a ball through a baby hoop in his granny's shit-sad backyard." She stretched and yawned, heading for the door. "It sucks, though, you know? In this state you've got these crazy extremes"—Sonya turned and started ticking them off on her fingers—"You've got your meth-addict poor people, your rich-as-balls horse people, a whole buncha regular people just trying to find or keep a job—"

"Okayokayokay." I shook my head, trying to clear it. What happened to our merry little conversations about boys? "Sonya, where's this going?"

"The point is that black or white, rich or poor, whatever—the one single stupid thing everyone seems to have in common is a maniacal love for basketball. Am I right?"

I thought of GoGo, her crossword puzzles and her basketball. "Yeah. Strange but true."

"So it sucks to ruin that one good thing with a big fight about coal. It's like drawing a line and telling everyone to pick a side. Kevin doesn't want to pick a side; he just wants to play ball. It's what he was born to do, and it's what he's going to do." Sonya paused to look at Jessica's photo display on her way out. She had this look of sad fondness on her face, like Jessica was someone she had known a hundred years ago.

"Sonya. Wait. What are you going to do?"

Sonya paused in the doorway, her hip resting against the frame. "What, you mean right now?"

"When you graduate."

"Girl, why do you think I'm here? I'm gonna take that UK scholarship and run like a bat outta hell before somebody changes their mind. Scholarships don't exactly grow on trees where I come from."

"Really," I said. "Because the trees in Louisville are covered in scholarships. Scholarships, money, chocolate. Take your pick. La-La Land is crawling with stuff you wouldn't believe."

Sonya managed a smile. "Touché." She chewed at a fingernail and looked at me for real. "Seriously, though, Glo. What are you going to do?"

"I don't know," I said. I opened GoGo's book and studied her handwritten signature. Same name as mine. "What do you think of New York City?"

Sonya shrugged. "Never been. But I get sick of everybody acting like there's California, and then there's New York, and nothing worthwhile happens in between. There's a whole huge fascinating country in between, is what there is."

"True."

"Well, we can make it true, or we can just be dicks." Sonya sighed and gave me her sad-fond smile. "G'night, Glo. How about we all start over tomorrow?"

Sonya left so quietly that I didn't even hear the door click shut behind her. I wasn't used to a quiet Sonya, and even I, self-proclaimed lover of silence and solitude, felt uneasy in the stillness that settled over the room. Shame, blame: I couldn't put my finger on the exact feeling welling up in me, but I knew I felt awful. Awful because what had

I done throughout my high-school career but perform in silly plays and work at a silly coffee shop so I could blow all my money on music? So I could flail my body around at shows and drive around in my dead grandmother's car and stare at the river and dream about an impossible boy? I curled myself into an even tighter ball, squeezed my eyes shut, assessing the damage: Jessica was right. In addition to never having thought about the mountains of Eastern Kentucky before that morning, I had also, just an example, never picked a blackberry, never planted a tree or taken the time to help something grow, never wanted for anything for one second of my life, blahblahblah, the list went on and on, the list made me sick, the list smacked of privilege and indulgence and general sanctimonious cluelessness. I felt awful because I loved Jessica and Sonya and was already missing them, because our misunderstandings felt seismic, because it seemed that things were always coming to an end before they even had a chance to begin.

For once in my life, I didn't want to be alone.

My hands were unsteady as I dug in my bag for the calling card. My father picked up on the first ring.

"Hi, Dad."

A pause, during which I could practically hear my father bracing himself. This particular brand of call was not exactly new to him.

"Well, hello there, Glo."

"Dad."

"Gloria?"

"Yes. Hi. Hello."

"Is everything all right?"

The tears were traveling my sinuses now, threatening histrionics. "Yes. Everything's fine. I love it here, but the food is really bad. So hey, do you know anything about mountaintop removal? The Coal Coalition? All that?"

Dad waited. I could hear the TV going in the background. *Antiques Roadshow.* "Well, of course I do," he said. Then he paused, gauging. "Gloria, what is this about?"

"I just wondered what you thought about it, that's all."

Another pause. "Gloria. Why don't you tell me what you think about it?"

"I think it's *terrible*," I wailed, crying full-on.

Dad waited for me to cry a little bit more before he continued. "Gloria, honey, you're the only one who can decide what you think and how you feel about things. The important thing is to always think things through. Think before you speak." He paused, tentative. "I'm grasping at straws here, honey—am I on the right track?"

My dad has always been able to do that—to read my mind that way, even when I'm all over the map. It's a trick he inherited from GoGo, Mind Reader Extraordinaire. "Everything's fine," I said, blinking hard, pulling it together. "Dad?"

"Hmm?"

"How come you never took me to pick blackberries?"

Dad sighed. I was wearing him out. "It sounds like you need a good night's sleep, Gloria. Things will be clearer in the morning, I promise. Call me tomorrow if you need to, but if I know you, you won't need to. I'll see you in a few weeks. I guarantee I'll be the last person on earth you'll want to see."

I smiled. My father, the original prophet-seer. "I love you, Dad."

"Remain calm."

"I will."

I must have fallen asleep, because all of a sudden there was the rude gleam of a flashlight in my face.

"Hey!" I screamed.

"Glo, get up," Jessica whispered. "Flashlight tag!"

I was still half dreaming as Jessica led me by the arm into the startling fluorescence of the hallway, down two dizzying flights of stairs, and into the warm breath of the night. Fireflies were rising up in luminescent drifts from the dark expanse of lawn, and everywhere flashlights blinked on and off, trailing laughter. Jessica's hair shone in the moonlight and disappeared in a wave behind her as she made for the Kissing Tree, the swing. I was aware of the grass beneath my bare feet as I ran after her—I was aware of the shadows, the moonlight, the night air on my

162

skin, humming magic. The disorientation of a moment before gave way to giddiness; I was laughing and couldn't stop, I was nine years old again, flying down the hill on my bike. I was vaguely aware of being alone—Jessica and the others had disappeared, but lights were still winking in the trees, so I ran for the swing and set myself sailing.

"I surrender!" I screamed, just to see how far my voice would go. And it did feel like surrendering: to the game, the night, the delicious freedom of it all.

"You're it," Mason whispered, appearing from nowhere and catching me in his light. "Boo."

"Boo who?"

"Boo Radley, at your service."

Mason switched off the light. I stared at his silhouette until my eyes got used to the dim and his face, suddenly nearer, came into focus.

"Kind of ruins the surprise," he murmured. "I obviously didn't think I'd run into you here."

"Really? I'd have thought only you could arrange a midnight game of flashlight tag."

Mason shrugged. "I have to admit this is not my work."

It occurred to me that all conversations with boys should happen this way: in whispers, bathed in moonlight. Everyone looks beautiful in the moon.

"What's in the tree, though, that is my work," Mason continued. "In the style of Weegee, just for you."

I turned to investigate the hole in the tree, but Mason reached out to stop me. His touch wasn't anything, really, just barely enough pressure to get my attention, but I felt it at the bottom of my stomach: a blue butterfly set free. "Wait'll I'm gone. Leave some of the surprise as a surprise."

"I promise that I could not possibly be more surprised," I admitted, still whispering, just for the thrill of it. Then he turned to go, loping up the hill.

Back in room 317, I took pains not to wake Jessica, who had somehow beaten me home and fallen asleep in a fully clothed heap on her bed. Moonlight slanted through the window and rested on her face and hair, which spilled over the pillow in a fairy-tale whorl. As gently as I could, I slipped the flip-flops from her feet, drew the top sheet over her legs, and picked up the flashlight that she had let fall to the floor. My heart was thrumming as I fumbled for Indigo in the half-dark; I didn't feel prepared to open Mason's package without a sound track. Cocooned in the music, I could suspend myself in that moment of discovery—a moment I prolonged as long as I could before giving in completely to an anticipation that I felt as an actual ache in my cheeks, the ache of biting into something so sweet that the thrill of the sugar makes your face hurt.

I climbed under the covers and shone the flashlight on Mason's gift: a roll of something or somethings, bound in string. I unfurled it to reveal an 8x10 black-and-white photograph. The girl in the picture was me. Me in the Mystery Machine, eyes locked with the eye of Mason's camera, mouth tilted in an incredulous smirk. It was the girl from the mirror, it was the girl from the wall in McGrath's tomb, it was the girl from the moon, as far away as that. A familiar girl with a faraway look in her eye. I'd know her anywhere; I didn't know her at all. Over her eyes Mason had outlined a pair of 3-D movie glasses—a nod to Weegee's 3-D-movie lovers, no doubt, although this girl—me, I—was alone, not locked in some passionate embrace. Underneath her/my face, Mason had taped a fortune cookie message: *One who admires you greatly is hidden before your eyes.* God! He almost had me. So if I was the 3-D girl with hidden eyes, did he think I was *his* admirer? *Oh, Mr. Mad Hatter,* I thought. *How fearfully wrong thou art.* I set the photo aside to assess page 2: a purple flyer like the one that had appeared in my campus mailbox several days before. It was an announcement. A call for participants in the end-of-Geek-Camp talent show. Was he serious? On principle, I had never—and would never, especially not with Mason—participate in something as fourth-grade ridiculous as that. Beneath all the flyer-411, Mason had scrawled *Much Ado I.i: Come on. You'd be perfect: "I had rather hear my dog bark at a crow than a man swear he loves me."—Beatrice/Gloria*

I shoved the photograph and the flyer underneath my pillow and decided to sleep on it, literally. I was finished with acting, but the single line of Shakespearean prose was another lit match, quick and hot.

"Glo?"

I turned to see Jessica facing me, her eyes glistening in the arc of moonlight that stretched across her bed and her face. "Yeah?"

"I'm sorry. For before. For those things I said."

"I'm sorry, too. I wasn't thinking. I didn't know— "

"It's okay. You don't have to say anything else. Please just don't say anything else." Jessica closed her eyes and curled herself into a ball. "I've never met anyone like you before, you know."

I wasn't sure what to do with that. What was I like?

"I mean you're different. You're so weird. Good-weird, though." Jessica sniffed. She may have been crying, but I wasn't sure. As far as I was concerned there had been enough crying for one night.

"And I'm not," Jessica continued, "I'm not going to go changing my mind about you just because we disagree about stuff."

"Okay," I said. "So my weird shoes are okay with you?"

"I still think your shoes are hideous."

"What about your hideous boat shoes? Hello, land-locked state."

"Hey," Jessica said, laughing. "Don't knock the boat shoes. They're iconic Americana, man."

"No, man, my Chucks are iconic Americana."

Jessica was smiling, her hands tucked beneath her head. "That's us, Glo. Opposite ends of the iconic-Americana spectrum."

"We should be models," I said.

"We should," Jess said dreamily.

I thought of my first moments in room 317, how I'd looked at those pictures of Jessica and made up my mind about her before she'd even had a chance to be her flesh-and-blood real-life self. I thought of how the room looked to me then, and how the days and nights had transformed it into a different place altogether. It had been changed by the living we'd done in it, the secrets we had spilled into it through wee-hour talks in the dark, just like this one.

Jessica propped her head up on one hand, examining the fingers of her other hand in the silver light. "Hey, did you get something from Alex?"

"This? No, this isn't from Alex. This, if you can believe it, is courtesy of the Mad Hatter."

Jessica laughed. "I think you secretly love him."

"Who? Alex? No kidding."

"Not Alex. The Mad Hatter. I'm not an Alex fan, I have to say."

I rose up on my elbows, balking. "What's wrong with Alex? You've never even met him."

"I don't need to meet him. It just seems like if he were

really into you, if he really appreciated you, he wouldn't keep your romance some big secret."

"We don't have a romance—"

"Precisely," Jessica interrupted. She tucked her hands back beneath her head and gave me an apologetic smile. "Girl, I know you love that CD, but a CD's not love. Love of the chickenshit variety, maybe, but you deserve to be swept off your feet in the here and now. That's all I'm saying."

"I don't want to be swept off my feet," I said. *I had rather hear my dog bark at a crow than a man swear he loves me.*

"Whatever, Glo." Jessica yawned, drifting. "Dude, I will give you a million dollars if you get up and shut the blinds. Get that crazy moon out of my eyes."

I climbed out of bed and shut the blinds against the light of the moon, but not before my mind took a picture of it, *click*. In seconds or minutes, it would be July, but in those final moments of the last day of June, I knew for sure I had been handed one of those days—an ordinary, extraordinary Favorite Day. I had cried but outdone my crying with laughing, and although the day was shot through the middle with pain, it was lit, in the end, with grace. The kind of day when you say to yourself, *That was it, that's when it happened, that's when I understood.* The kind of day to play on repeat behind your eyes at night.

11

Reply Hazy, Try Again

Dear Alex,

Thanks for the CD! I love it. How's the Land of
the Midnight Sun? I've been thinking

Hey Alex,

So how are you? How's the Last Frontier? I listen
to the CD all the time and

Hello, Alexander.

You are so right: That U2 recording is epic. I
never knew there were so many songs with my name
in them. Geek Camp is interesting but

To: Alex

From: Gloria, i.e. She Who Is Not Yet Out of Your System, Remember Moi???

Hey. Look at me, writing with actual pen and paper! Geek Camp has been a learning experience in more ways than six. In addition to gaining an appreciation for dogs and small children I've also

ALEX ALEX ALEX WTF WTF WTF WTF WTF????????????!!!!!!!!!!!!!!!!

Here's the thing about writing letters: You have to be in the mood for that stuff. I'd started about four million letters to Alex but hadn't finished any of them. Maybe Jessica was right. Maybe Alex was a bad idea. My confusion was only compounded by the general air of *amour* that had suddenly settled over Morlan like some sort of sticky, cotton-candy fog: Geek Camp wasn't even halfway over and relationships were sprouting up—and in some cases had already bloomed and died—all over the place. It was mystifying, entertaining, and gross. The Kissing Tree had lost its charm; the whole campus had become one big Kissing Tree, with people making out indiscriminately around every corner and beneath every eave.

"New rule," Chloe said, eyeing us over a chocolate milk shake. "Nobody at this table is going to go out, make out, or otherwise dally romantically with anybody else at this table. Got it?"

Calvin nodded brightly. I shot him a look. "Way to be enthusiastic about rejecting us, there, Cal."

"I'm all for friendship," Calvin said. "It's the way to go."

"Chloe, does this mean we're breaking up?" Mason intoned in mock-horror. Chloe blew her straw wrapper at him. "Please," she said. "You are so not my type."

"What's wrong with me?"

"Well, you're a guy, for one thing."

This overdue bit of information hovered lightly above the table for a second and finally caught on Calvin's left eyebrow, which hitched ever so slightly.

"Congratulations, Cal," Chloe grinned. "You're actual, true friends with a real-life lesbian. You did it without even trying!"

Calvin blushed deeper than ever. "Cool," he said.

"So what brought this on?" Mason asked, distracted as usual. He was busy photographing the contents of Chloe's bag. On the table, lined up in a neat row, he had arranged a silver skull ring, a cough drop, a tube of mascara, and a Magic 8 Ball, which Chloe told us she had purchased for fifty cents at the legendary World's Longest Yard Sale. *Still Life with Chloe's Luggage.*

"What brought what on? The gay thing?"

"No, the rule thing."

Chloe sighed and gazed skyward. "I just think this campus has gone nuts, that's all. I mean, my roommate's been preaching the gospel at me since the second I met her, trying to save my soul and all that, but she doesn't seem to mind falling into bed with Eric."

"Wait a minute. Eric the resident adviser?"

"Eric the RA." Chloe nodded. "Twenty-year-old Eric the RA, he of the overzealous spray tan. But don't worry, it's cool, it's a *God Match*."

Nervously, I scanned Calvin's and Mason's faces for signs of agitation. The conflict with Jessica and Sonya was still heavy on my conscience, and I worried that our little foursome might implode in the face of someone's hidden religious agenda. GoGo was right: It is not wise to go around casually yak-yakking about religion and politics. I picked up Chloe's 8 Ball and gave it a shake. *Reply Hazy, Try Again.*

"A God Match," Mason repeated. "Sounds incendiary."

Calvin shifted uncomfortably and rubbed his eyes. "Talking about God, it's like trying to . . . I don't know. It's like trying to catch a blue butterfly. To nail something beautiful like that to the wall." Calvin paused to sip from his milk. I exchanged a glance with Chloe: This was an example of what the two of us had started referring to as a "Calvinism"; i.e., the sort of startling kernel of wisdom and deep feeling that Calvin would quietly toss out after any number of minutes or hours of complete silence. The boy contained multitudes. "My roommate wants me to go to church with him next Sunday," he continued. Church. I kept forgetting that Geek Camp provided us with the option of worshipping at the college's chapel on Sundays.

"Are you gonna go?" Chloe asked. "Because you know, you guys can always come to visit me in God's very own Boone County. Never mind that the place is named for a freaking historically immortal fron*tiers*man; now our claim to fame is the Creation Museum! Come one, come all to see the Bible in megatronic, supersonic—"

"Chloe," Calvin said evenly, "are you going to let me talk? I mean, are you going to let me answer your question or not?"

"I'm sorry," Chloe said, chastened. We watched her rummage in her brain for a second. "What'd I ask you, again?"

"Am I going to church with my roommate next Sunday."

"Right. Well. Are you?"

Calvin shrugged. "Why not? Maybe I'll learn something. Then maybe I can take him to my church, see what he thinks."

Chloe's steel trap of a mind seized on that immediately. "Wait a minute. Didn't you tell us a while back, right here at this table, that you don't *go* to church?"

"The farm," Calvin said, clear-eyed, direct. It was the most confident I'd ever seen him be with us. "That's my church."

Nobody said anything for a few seconds, and Calvin rapped his knuckles on the table, two swift wrap-'em-up knocks. "Let's go," he said. "I've got to go pick up Holyfield."

Holyfield, as it turned out, had all but officially become Calvin's dog. Somehow X had managed to keep his job despite what Jessica had claimed were his attempts to brainwash us, and—perhaps most significantly—despite his having basically pawned his dog off on Calvin Little. Our own Calvin, with his needlepoint belts and immaculate manners, had succeeded in convincing all the in-charge types over at the boys' dorm that Holyfield was not only an important lesson in caretaking and responsibility, but also a noble and respectable mascot. Everybody loved Holyfield, and Holyfield, in turn, had increased everybody's love for Calvin, the skinny redheaded dude who didn't say much but had managed to break all the rules through the devilishly clever move of appearing to be the sort of person who would never, ever dream of breaking the rules.

"So what's your roommate have to say about that dog?" Chloe asked as we made our way to class, Holyfield in tow.

"One of God's creatures," Calvin grinned. "What would Saint Francis do?"

X had agreed to hold class outdoors, and we found him where he said he'd be: dozing beneath the Kissing Tree. Holyfield beelined for his face and slathered it with slobbery Holyfield love. "How's he doing?" X asked Calvin.

"Fine," Calvin said. "We get along."

"This is just a trial period, you do understand," X said, peering at Calvin over his glasses. Then Holyfield broke everybody's heart by looking from one to the other of them, old dad to new dad, confused. He cocked his head and waited for something to happen.

"Holyfield, buddy, come here," Calvin said softly. The dog perked up his ears, trotted up to Calvin, and rolled onto his back, tongue lolling goofily from the corner of his mouth.

"Trial period, my arse," X said. "Calvin, my man, looks like you've got yourself a dog. Also, you're on. The stage is yours. Knock us out. Everybody else: Lend Calvin your ears and your full attention, please. This is serious business."

As we made ourselves comfortable in the shade of the tree, Calvin shuffled to a standing position before us. His face and the tips of his ears were fully aflame. In his hands he rotated a neat stack of index cards. "Okay," he breathed. "Um, okay." He cleared his throat a couple of times, and Mason elbowed me to look at something he had scrawled in his notebook: *What about the talent show?* I shook my head in a *not right now* warning just as Chloe thwacked me on the arm with a pencil.

"Ow!"

"Cal," Chloe said, giving me the evil eye, "we're listening. Remember, it's just us. You can tell us anything, right?" She took a drag from her pencil, scooped up Holyfield, and gathered him into her lap. "Here," she said. "Forget about us. Forget we're here. Just talk right to Holyfield, okay?"

Dutifully, Holyfield perked up his ears. He kneaded his little white sock-paws into Chloe's skirt as if he were cozying himself up to hear a good story. I'm telling you: Holyfield was absolutely the coolest dog I'd ever met in my life. He could make a convert out of anyone.

"Okay," Calvin said. "Okay." He stared down at his index cards and took a shaky breath. In that moment I could sense Calvin's nervousness so keenly that I almost got up and ran, just to free us all. It's like when you go to a play and an actor falters—even if it's just a line, just a single word, the veil comes crashing down and it's so excruciating and embarrassing that you just want to *la la la!* squinch your eyes shut and pretend yourself back to the safety of the parking lot. I mean, I know it was just us, sitting around in the sunshine waiting for Calvin to talk about some book, but the performance anxiety was killing me; it was catching; my armpits were dampening on Calvin's behalf. *Cal,* I prayed, *get it together.* Then he looked up at us, eyes a clear and steady blue. "My Great American Novel is called *Nathan Coulter,* and it could be the story of my life."

It was just like in that movie, the one where they put on the play and the guy with the stage fright is responsible for the opening speech of the first-ever performance of *Romeo and Juliet:* You're cringing and dying, thinking the guy won't get over his stammer, that the play will be a failure, and then he comes out with it—*Two households, both alike in dignity*—with such nobility and strength of purpose that you're already hooked, you're already crying, and Gwyneth Paltrow and her doomed lover haven't even appeared on the scene yet.

I had never the hell even *heard* of Calvin's book, but as he stood beneath that ancient sycamore, explaining to us why he loved it, reading a passage from it with genuine conviction and gaining confidence as he read, I fell for him a little bit, just for a second: the rogue lock of red hair that the breeze kept blowing into his eyes, the pale down on his neatly sinewed arms—arms that I could suddenly (ridiculously) imagine hefting firewood, cradling newborn babies, commandeering wheelbarrows and other farm paraphernalia. *Conviction,* that was the word—it was that belief in, that *loyalty* to, a thing. I had been surprised—no, awed—to see it all over the place at Geek

Camp. I mean, I couldn't fathom how someone could look at the ruins of a mountain and see it as anything other than a crime, but for Jessica it was linked to things she would defend with her life: her family, her hometown, her history, her future. She thought I was weird and had said so out loud, but I had no doubt that her loyalty to me — to anyone she befriended — was fierce and final.

Jessica and Sonya, they had it all figured out: They were going to stay in Kentucky and become lawyers and, like Calvin, give something back to the place that had raised them. I myself could barely see past the dreamscape of next week . . . What did I want? Unexpected magic. To get swept up and carried away, daily and maybe forever, by the powerful undertow of music and books. I marveled that I had ever landed at Geek Camp to begin with — I didn't have the grades or the ambition or the drive, I was beginning to realize. I was lazy. Lazy and given to paroxysms of boy-craziness that I would have denied with a furious passion if you'd asked me. I did seem to be armed with a sort of pathological thirst for learning stuff, but that's just it: The *learning* was what got me. The business of learning-as-a-means-to-an-end? Well. That eluded me completely. I was hopeless. Destined to be broke and brokenhearted.

"So if the Great American Novel is linked, somehow, to the American Dream," Calvin was saying, "then my dream is to honor the land. Let it teach me what it has to teach me. Not just me. All of us." He squinted down at us, holding his breath. "That's all, I guess."

Chloe, eyes glistening, let go of Holyfield so she could applaud. X rose from the ground and clapped Calvin on the shoulder. "That was excellent, Calvin," he said. "I'm proud of you." He removed his glasses and started cleaning them with the bottom of his T-shirt. "I'm proud of all of you, actually," he said to the ground, to no one in particular. "Do you know why I sent those letters home, asking yall to get yourselves unplugged for a month?"

By now Calvin had joined us on the ground, curled in a lanky fermata around Holyfield. Chloe had spread a quilt on the grass and we were all heaped there in the sun, laughing and congratulating Cal. In that moment the love I felt for each one of them rose up in me so quickly I had to blink—hard—to keep it from spilling out my eyes.

"It doesn't matter, really," X continued, "but I just didn't want to contend with all that noise. It was my litmus test. I wanted to see what kind of students I'd get if I handed you some arbitrary rule like that."

I remembered Carol, how she'd said we'd get a chocolate factory in the end. I made a mental note to write her about this decidedly Wonka development.

"I started out with twenty-three takers, and after the letter went home, it was just you four," X said. "Can you believe that? Most of the complaints came from parents, not kids."

Mason visored his eyes with his hand. Something in him had shifted in the space of a blink. "So what are you saying, X? Spit it out."

"I guess I'm just glad things worked out the way they did," X said, shrugging amiably. "You're a good group, a good group."

For some reason, this upended Mason. "Well, maybe we are and maybe we aren't," he said, standing and dusting himself off. "Maybe that remains to be seen, right? Maybe your little litmus test wasn't quite comprehensive enough."

"Mason," Chloe said softly. She rested her hand on his shoe. "Dude."

"I mean, are we going to have class, or what?" Mason angled his blue gaze on X. "Are you going to teach this class, or are we going to sit around and sing 'Kumbaya' and maybe pack a big fat bowl?"

X, like the rest of us, was visibly taken aback. "Let's have class," he said carefully. "And you're welcome to leave if that doesn't suit."

Mason blinked, holding his ground. "I'm not leaving."

"Good," X said.

Everybody sat there, breath suspended, hoping Mason was finished. He wasn't.

"I'm also not ever going to be anybody's *pawn*. Not yours, not anybody's. Okay?"

X waited to see if Mason had anything else to say. "Okay," he said. "Mason. You're not a pawn. I didn't mean it that way. You're an important part of this class, is what you are. You're also up next. Have you picked a Great American Novel to present to us?"

"No," Mason said, quieter now. "No, I haven't decided yet." He sat back down, elbows to knees, ankles crossed, folding himself in. "Stay tuned."

Holyfield, our very own Emotional Barometer, settled himself next to Mason and heaved an empathetic sigh, crinkling his puppy-eyebrow tufts in sympathy. Mason stroked his ears and spoke to him gently. "Whatup, little bro. How about you don't chew on my shoe?"

X cleared his throat and stroked his beard. It was disconcerting, the way he seemed so scared of us sometimes. *Just be in charge!* I wanted to scream. *Own the authority! Grow some balls!* Seriously, is it too much to ask to find one single teacher in this world to look up to? Just one? Some part of me had clicked along with Mason's sudden mood shift; I couldn't say exactly what it was, but a thread of understanding had passed between the two of us.

X had started talking again—this time about Henry James—and I scribbled a note to Mason: *Okay, I'm in.* I elbowed him and tilted my notebook so he could see. "Excellent," he whispered, and winked—a wink that, despite everything, sent a blue butterfly free-falling through my stomach. Immediately, I thought to change my mind, but it was already in writing: I was going to enter that stupid talent show alongside the Mad Hatter. Un-freaking-believable.

Chloe was dutifully taking notes as X waxed enthusiastic about *The Portrait of a Lady*. I nudged her and motioned for the Magic 8 Ball, which had rolled out of her bag and was gleaming like a promise in the sun. With a decidedly schoolmarm-ish frown (I know! Chloe! Getting all dutiful and prim!), she handed it over. I conjured my question in my head and shook the ball in what I considered impressively surreptitious fashion —

"Gloria? It appears you're in possession of some fascinating news over there. If it's so much more fascinating than Isabel Archer, kindly share it with the rest of us."

Embarrassment rose up in me like heat rash. "No, that's okay."

"What do you mean, *that's okay*?" X shook his head and let out a mocking laugh. "Your generation is something else. Would you like another Coke? *No, I'm okay.* What happened to *No, thank you*? Basic manners? Kindergarten stuff? You're okay. I'm glad you're okay. Are you okay enough to pay attention?"

I nodded. For all the bullshit airs I put on about being a rebellious soul, I can't stand to be called out like that. Here was X, acting like a teacher just when I was hoping he would, but I was too mortified to fully appreciate the moment.

"So what've you got there? Enthrall us, please, with the unparalleled acumen of the Eight Ball."

The blue liquid had cleared to reveal its watery triangle of wisdom: *Better Not Tell You Now.*

12

Krispy Kreme and
the Goddess of Wisdom

IF WONDERLAND'S White Queen was indeed capable of believing six impossible things before breakfast, it should be said of me that I was—am—fully capable of falling in love even more times before breakfast than that. It's like a disease. X had sent us home with a big chunk of *The Portrait of a Lady*, and almost immediately I had fallen head over heels for poor, soulful Ralph Touchett, the invalid cousin of Isabel Archer (who, in my opinion, needed a swift kick in the ass). X's curriculum made absolutely no sense at all; he just jumped around from book to book, author to author, Europe to America, just gush-gush-gushing about the power of words and hoping, I guess, that some of his enthusiasm would stick. Later that summer (school looming ominously on the calendar, the promise of fall infusing the air with nostalgia itself, you know the mood), it would hit me: It would occur to me that X *had* reached us; that Geek Camp would forever mark for me the point in my life when I discovered that words are alchemy, that words really can save us.

On Fourth of July morning, though, I wasn't thinking about any of that. I was lazing in bed, swooning over Ralph Touchett while Jessica snored lightly in the opposite bed. In honor of the holiday it was also Parents' Day, which meant that the hours of nine to noon would be open to any parents who wanted to visit their kids. Diane showed up at 8:30 with a box of Krispy Kreme doughnuts and a freshly lacquered French manicure that made her fingernails look like the squared-off ends of screwdrivers.

"Yoo-hoo!"

Jessica opened one eye and rolled back over. "Mom, you're early."

I climbed out of bed and stood up. "Hi, Mrs. Dixon. I'm Gloria." I offered my hand.

Diane looked me briskly up and down and stuck the doughnut box into my outstretched hand. "Nice to meet you, Gloria."

I selected my favorite: a chocolate-iced cream-filled. "Wow, thank you. Jess, you want one?"

Jessica swung her legs over the side of the bed and stretched. "Mmmm," she said, reaching for the box.

"Ah-ah-ah," Diane sang, tapping the back of Jessica's hand with a screwdriver. "Let's not forget our diet, honey."

I looked from Diane to Jessica, confused. "So these are all for me?"

Diane beamed. "Enjoy!"

Jessica rubbed her eyes and gathered up her shower stuff. "Mom," she said, "just let me get dressed. I'll meet you in the lobby as soon as I'm done. How's that sound?"

Diane looked pointedly at her watch and heaved a sigh. "Well get a move on, honey. So much shopping to do, so little time!"

The door clicked shut and I looked at Jessica, aghast. I waited for her to cry, which is what I would have done, but instead she blithely tore into a caramel doughnut. I couldn't decide which was more shocking: Diane herself, or Jessica's apparent immunity to her. "Ibbour dad cubbing?" Jess mumbled through a mouthful of crumbs.

I shook my head. "I begged him not to."

"Do you want to come to the mall with us? There's this early-bird holiday sale thing."

Was she serious? Can you say *nightmare*? "I think I'll stay here and work on my presentation," I said.

Jessica smiled. "Well, if you change your mind in

the next twenty minutes, just holler. You're invited." She cocked her head at me so I'd know she meant it.

"Thanks, but I'm glad for the quiet. It's perfect."

On her way out the door, Jessica switched off the overhead light. "Coal keeps the lights on," she sang as she disappeared toward the bathroom. It was a familiar refrain: ever since our little disagreement, she'd been getting a huge kick out of plunging the room into darkness, taping little notes over the light switch and across the refrigerator door: *Coal keeps the fridge on, bitches!*

She wasn't going to sway me anytime soon. "I love you, too!" I called out after her. "Bye!"

The quiet really was awesome. It felt restorative, like sleep or good food. I basked in it, in the glow of doomed and beautiful Ralph Touchett, as I listened to the bustle outside the door: parents reuniting with their kids, planning their mornings. I chewed on a coconut doughnut and contemplated the absolute gorgeousness of solitude.

Then the phone rang. I sensed who it was before I picked up.

"Mason?"

Pause.

I tried again. "Mason?"

"Holy shit, how'd you do that?"

I grinned. "Sixth sense."

The sweetness of my impromptu breakfast, the

chocolaty sound of Mason's surprised voice: My heart was on a sugar high. "So what's up?"

"Your parents coming?"

Pause. "Nope. Yours?"

Pause. "Nope." Another pause. "Want to meet me in the auditorium in an hour? You know, to take a look at the script?"

I examined the coconut piled on my doughnut, imagined reading the pieces like tea leaves. Where was Chloe's 8 Ball when I needed it?

"Okay," I said, hoping I sounded nonchalant.

"Are you eating something?"

"A coconut doughnut."

"You shouldn't talk with your mouth full. It's rude." I could hear him smiling through the phone.

"Good*bye*, Mason."

I hung up the phone and spent the next five minutes suspended somewhere in the emotional no-man's-land between giddiness and fury, jumping up and down and spinning around the room, trying to shake up my heart like a Magic 8 Ball, hoping I'd be able to look in the mirror and see the answer to my question revealed in my face: What, exactly, was happening to me?

The auditorium looked different—bigger—with nobody in it. My footsteps echoed throughout the darkened hall as I walked across the polished wood of the stage. Above me, the lights dozed on their tracks, all but one: a single spotlight angling a gentle column of light on center stage. I breathed in the familiar smell of paint—paint mixed with dust and anticipation. It was like returning home after a vacation and being reminded, as soon as you enter the door, that your house has a distinct *home*-smell, a smell that's as much a part of your house—of you—as brick and mortar, as breathing.

I stepped into the light and let my bag fall to the floor. There were the empty seats, stretched in rows before me, holding their breath. Just to remember what it felt like, just to see if I still had it, I set my voice free, a blue butterfly fleeing the net: "*'Open your ears; for which of you will stop the vent of hearing when loud Rumour speaks?'*"

Three slow claps resounded from somewhere in the dark room. My heart echoed each of them with a reverberating *thud*.

I shaded my eyes, peering into the dark. "Mason?"

"Henry Four, Part Two," said Mason's disembodied voice. "Very impressive."

Thud, thud. "Where are you?"

"Up here."

I looked up to find Mason sitting on the catwalk, swinging his legs, pointing his camera at me. Suddenly self-conscious, I folded my arms across my chest. "How long have you been up there?"

"Long enough to get to watch you while you didn't know I was watching."

I swallowed, hard. "Get down here."

With a grace that wasn't lost on me, Mason traversed the catwalk and climbed down an impossibly narrow spiral staircase concealed at the rear of the wings. "Hi," he said, joining me in the pool of light.

"Hi." I shifted from one leg to the other and finally decided to sit cross-legged on the floor. I was having trouble looking him in the eye. "Let's get started."

"Okay." Mason settled down, mirroring my pose. His left knee touched my right just barely.

I scooted back. "No camera," I said.

"Fine." Mason stuck the camera in his bag, from which he drew two copies of the script. "Here."

I glanced at the pages. The words were swimming. "So do you want to do a quick read-through before we block the scene or what?"

Mason tapped his teeth with his fingernail. An obnoxious habit. "Let's warm up first."

I rolled my eyes. Surely he wasn't going to make me do vocal exercises, *red-leather-yellow-leather* and all that bulsh.

"Seriously, this isn't going to work unless we get the trust down first. I mean, let's face it. You can't stand me, right?"

My eyes flicked up and met Mason's head-on. "I can stand you just fine. Most of the time."

"Good. Hold out your hands. Palms up, like this."

I raised my eyebrows, a bitchy little warning.

"Jesus, Gloria. I'm not going to bite you. Just hold out your hands, okay? Good. Now close your eyes."

I complied, waiting for Mason to deposit something disgusting in my hands. A used piece of gum, maybe, or a dead roach. I wouldn't have put it past him.

"Keep your eyes closed. Don't cheat!"

"Okay."

With my eyes closed, my other senses ramped up: From somewhere in the building I could hear the rich, mournful lowing of a cello. I could smell the toothpaste on Mason's breath and the clean scent of his still-damp hair. A moment later I could feel the warmth of his palms, which hovered just above my own—not touching, but almost.

"Now," Mason said. "What's your favorite color?"

My eyes flew open and I started laughing. I couldn't help it. "What? I don't need my eyes closed for this!"

"Fine. Keep them open, but dude, don't *laugh*. Come on, this is serious. Get with it. Deep breath." Mason filled his lungs with air.

"Is this like that game where it's my job to slap the tops of your hands before you have a chance to move them away? Because I suck at that game, and I'm not into violence."

Mason dropped his shoulders and took his hands back. "Gloria. Come on. Are you with me here or not? You gotta focus."

"Okay okay okay." I sat up straight. "I'm focusing. Starting now."

We realigned our palms and took a couple of simultaneous breaths. I have this horrible condition where nervousness equals inappropriate laughter, so I had to fight the urge to crack up. I decided to focus my eyes on a tiny scar on Mason's temple. "What happened there?"

"My scar? Forceps. Doctor had to yank me out. My mom says I've been hard to handle ever since."

I grinned. Involuntarily. The spotlight buzzed faintly as it cast its glow on us.

"My turn," Mason said. "Do you have any scars?"

"Literal or figurative?"

"Either one. Doesn't matter."

My outstretched arms were starting to ache. My eyes were starting to water with the effort of keeping them locked with Mason's eyes, which seemed to throb in and out of focus. If you say a word out loud enough times, it starts to lose its meaning; it was like that with Mason's face—as I stared at it, it began to lose its shape. It was all cool blue eyes and toothpaste. I became painfully aware of my contacts.

"I have plenty of scars," I said finally. "But I'll live."

"Your turn," Mason said. The heat between our palms felt like one of those shimmery black mirages you see on the street when it's really hot outside.

"Okay," I said. "Why are you here instead of with your parents?"

"You mean parent?" Mason corrected. "My mom has better things to do. Besides, it kind of defeats the purpose, doesn't it? If you send your kid off to camp, you shouldn't have to deal with him until he comes home at the end. A month is not forever. Mid-month reunion? It's stupid. I'm not on board."

I nodded in agreement. "So where's your dad?"

"It's not your turn," Mason whispered.

"Sorry," I whispered back, stifling a giggle. My palms quivered reflexively and barely—just barely—kissed Mason's palms; *palm to palm is holy palmers' kiss*— God, my mind was Shakespeare-drunk; my mind was spinning.

Mason kept up with the whispering; his voice this time was barely audible. "Your eyes are grey. Like Grey-Eyed Athena. She's the goddess of wisdom, you know."

I rolled my grey eyes and really did laugh this time; I couldn't help it—it was maybe the loveliest thing anyone had ever said to me, and it was somehow important that I blow it off completely.

"That's not a question," I whispered.

193

"Oh yeah," Mason whispered. "So where are your parents?"

"You mean parent?" I made my voice as small as I could. Some part of me wished that Mason and I could have this conversation with eyes alone. Another part of me believed that we probably could. There weren't words for this stuff; whispering them into the dark was the way to go.

"My dad," I said, "stayed in Louisville because I asked him to."

Beneath Mason's hands, my hands were shaking.

"My mom," I whispered, "left the scene early on."

Mason's eyes traveled between mine, right-left, right-left. "Is she dead?"

"Nope," I whispered. "She is alive, in one piece, and absolutely gone."

Without a sound, Mason lowered his palms on top of mine. Our hands were sweaty. It was disgusting. It was the sweetest relief I'd ever felt in my life, and I felt it everywhere.

"That sucks," Mason murmured. "In a way, leaving's worse than dying. At least when somebody dies, people bring casseroles."

I laughed and wrapped my fingers around Mason's wrists. I could feel his quickening pulse beneath my thumbs. "Were there casseroles at your house?"

Mason nodded, a slow sad smile. "There were many,

many casseroles." He paused to swallow. "My dad, he left the scene early on, too. You know, orchestrated his own exit?"

I held Mason's gaze. Held tight to his hands.

"The worst part is how a lifetime of good things, hard work, happiness—it all gets eclipsed by this one bad day. He had a bad day, you know? One bad day out of thousands of good ones."

The truth hung between us like an incandescent bubble: Touch it and it shimmers away.

"Mason."

"Gloria?"

"My favorite color is blue."

We had an Egg Drop date with Chloe and Calvin at noon. As Mason and I emerged from the theater into the glare of midday, I felt empty-full and dazed, changed somehow, the way I feel when I step from the dark of a movie theater into the sunlit realm of real life. What had happened in there felt like a movie, like a thing Mason and I had watched happen to characters on a screen. Under the leafy canopy of trees lining the streets of campus, it seemed impossible that we had said those things out loud.

What I hadn't told Mason, though, is that my mother wasn't all bad. I don't really feel like going into all the things that were less than wonderful about her, but I'll tell you this: She had her moments, my mother. They weren't many, but they're enough. I'll take them, is what I'm saying. There was that baseball game, for instance, which I won't ever forget. There were radio songs sung loud and clear and happy in the car. Sometimes there were pancakes from scratch on Saturday mornings—those were unforgettable, too, and proof, in my mind, of a love that had to have been there. She just wasn't well, is what GoGo and my dad said. Sometimes people just aren't well, and it's nobody's fault, and there's no getting around it. One time Carol and I spent an entire afternoon stretched out on the floor with Carol's dad's *Diagnostic and Statistical Manual of Mental Disorders,* Fifth Edition, trying to figure out which one could be my mother. Bipolar Disorder, Narcissistic Personality Disorder, Intermittent Explosive Disorder: Each one was more plausible and entertaining than the last. "That's her exactly!" Carol and I screamed. We were cracking ourselves up. There was nothing funny about it, nothing even remotely funny at all, but Carol and I could not, could *not,* stop laughing. Merriment in the face of grief: It's what Carol's dad might refer to as a Defense Mechanism. Defense Mechanisms! People: They're my specialty. I'm trying to cut back, but it's harder than you might think.

Anyway. I'm a true professional when it comes to Mom-Shopping; I can evaluate other people's mothers in the blink of an eye. Maybe that's not very nice or generous of me, but there it is. It's an involuntary talent and

I've earned it. Mason had told me about his own fantastic mother, and it was clear that she belonged at one end of the spectrum, along with GoGo, Carol's mom, the mom from *Friday Night Lights,* and the best mom ever: my own dad. The opposite end was populated by the likes of my mother and the mom from *Ordinary People,* who in my opinion gets overlooked as one of *the* most frightening villains in all of American literature. Jessica's mom—who might as well have come into our room that morning waving a red flag—had earned a spot at the scary end of the spectrum. The more I thought about those doughnuts, the more I wanted to weep.

That's what I was thinking about as Mason and I walked along the sidewalk, a pair of orphans for the day: Diane's Krispy Kremes, and that playground singsong *Step on a crack, break your mother's back.* An innocuous rhyme that never fails to ring in my head every time I walk on a sidewalk—a stupid, small thing that can bring tears to my eyes on a bad day. I thought of Mason and his casseroles, Mason and his own complicated personal geometry; how everybody everywhere has some heartbreaking thing like my sidewalk rhyme. People and their multitudes. It just goes on and on, around and around. One of the things that had appealed to me about Geek Camp—about New York, about college—was the absence of parents, mine and everyone else's: We each had a chance at a clean slate. But then I arrived at Morlan and everybody was still glued to their parents via their stupid smartphones, and now the parents had broken the spell by descending on the place like a plague, and I had gone and lost my mind and spilled my guts to Mason Atkinson, of all people. My hands were shoved in my pockets, but I could still feel the imprint of his touch on my palms.

"Check it out," Mason said. He bent down and carefully drew a clover from the ground. "Four-leafer." He twirled it by the stem. "Here," he said. "You keep it."

I slid my bag down my arm and reached for the GBBoE. I held the book open while Mason pressed the clover between the pages.

"First one I've found in forever," Mason said. "I used to find them all the time, but then I started looking for them. You don't find half as many if you're looking for them."

"Nope," I agreed. The clover was there in my book, a perfect green charm. A tiny sign of wonder, storing up its good luck, awaiting its moment. What if the moment came and I missed it?

"Mason, I—"

"Shhh," he interrupted. "You don't have to say anything."

So I didn't.

Mason was right: I didn't have to.

⌒

"Closed for the holiday," Chloe announced from her spot on the ground. "Xiu Li has forsaken us, *mes amis*. Want some corn?"

Next to Chloe sat Calvin, and between them Holyfield was sniffing around in a bushel basket filled with vegetables. "Cal gave me a ride on the tractor," Chloe gushed. "And look at this. Basil! Doesn't it smell delicious?"

"The corn tastes good just like this," Calvin said. He shucked an ear with practiced ease and spun it between his fingers: The kernels were white and yellow together. "It's the best when it's fresh, when you don't do anything to it at all. Try it."

I accepted the ear from Calvin and took a tentative bite. The corn of my childhood was the frozen kind, boiled to death by my well-meaning dad, slathered in Parkay and balanced between a greasy set of those spiked, corn-shaped cob-holder things. Calvin's corn smelled like the earth and tasted like sunshine.

"This all came from your farm?"

Calvin nodded. "That variety's called Ambrosia."

Ambrosia. I love a word that casts its own spell, that sounds like what it's talking about, that tastes like the thing itself. If Ale-8 was the nectar of the gods, this corn was the fruit. The vegetable. Whatever. It made me want to cry.

Mason rubbed the basil between his fingers. "Potent stuff," he observed. "So Cal, why didn't Glo and I get invited to the farm?"

"Well, I invited myself at the last minute," Chloe confided. "We tried to call both of yall but nobody picked up. Right, Cal?"

"Yep," Calvin nodded. "Also, it didn't occur to me that everybody would get all revved up to spend a whole morning on a farm."

Calvin couldn't have been more wrong. The farm had taken on an enchanted glow in my mind—Narnia, Hogwarts, Calvin's Farm. I had already started to picture the four of us there in the fall, reuniting over marshmallows and a campfire.

"Your parents didn't come, either?" Mason asked Chloe.

"They're in Cozumel, if you can believe that. They were so excited to get rid of me that they had to flee the country in celebration."

It was good-natured, the way Chloe talked about her parents. There was love in her voice. Appreciation. I thought about X, about his litmus test. Maybe the real test hadn't been for us, but for our parents, and that by letting us go, they—we, all of us—had won. We had been handed the freedom to be who we wanted to be. It was better than a million chocolate factories. It was rare and wonderful. If I could just figure out who and what I wanted to be, it would be even better. I chewed my ear of sunshine and considered, for a second, my—our—excellent luck.

"So, Cal," I said. "Don't you have a brother? Does he work on the farm or what?"

Calvin shook his head. "Luke's older. About to start his third year at Berea."

"Calvin's parents are awesome," Chloe interrupted. "They're like the true freaking salt of the earth. You guys should've come."

"I was saying something," Calvin said, dazed. "Holyfield, what was I saying?"

The dog cocked his head, spun himself in a circle as if to think it over, and curled up next to Calvin's knee.

"Oh yeah," Cal said. "I was talking about my family. My parents aren't convinced I should take that scholarship. I mean, what're you guys gonna do?"

Chloe groaned. "The scholarship, the scholarship. I'm so sick of it. Can't we worry about that later? Can't I just please enjoy my senior year for a second?"

"I think I'm going to take it," Calvin said. He studied his corn, which he was eating in methodical, tidy rows. "Study agriculture. Get the degree. Once I earn it, nobody can ever take it away from me, you know?"

"Cal," I said, "you are the smartest person I know. You're going to have scholarships coming out of your ears, and not just from UK. Keep your options open."

"I want to be near the farm. That's what I know for sure. That's the only option for me."

I felt it again: that twinge of jealous awe at somebody having it all figured out. "Is the farm what *you* want for you, or what your parents want for you?"

"Are you kidding? My parents want me to go to Harvard and become a doctor."

Mason groaned. "Join the club."

"God, I think you need math for that," Chloe said. "Go with the farm, Cal. That place rocks."

"The good news is, they said I could keep Holyfield."

"Well, of course they did."

Holyfield seemed pleased.

Riiing.

The sound of the pay phone was so foreign to my ears that it may as well have been a siren. One of the Egg Drop's chief charms was that in so many ways it was a relic of a bygone era; I mean, there are probably something like, what, seven pay phones still in existence across the globe? The Egg Drop had the monopoly on not one but two of them: one on either side of the entrance. Mason was standing at the left one, patiently holding the phone to his ear. "Are yall going to pick up or what?"

"I can hear you from right here," Chloe said, stating the obvious. Mason ignored her, and the phone on the right continued to blare its dinosaur ring. Calvin gave me a pointed glance, so I eye-rolled my way to the receiver and picked up.

"Egg Drop Café, may I help you?"

"Yes. May I speak to Gloria Bishop, please?"

I flipped Mason the bird. "Speaking."

"Gloria! How's it going?"

"Um, super. How's it going with you?"

"Lemme talk to Chloe for a sec. Put her on."

Chloe and Calvin had just settled down to a pint of fresh-picked blackberries. "Tell him my mouth is full," Chloe said over her shoulder.

"Her mouth is full."

"So are we going to take the bus or hitch a ride with X? What's the plan?"

I had almost forgotten: We and the rest of the Geek Campers were supposed to be field-tripping it to Louisville for a riverfront concert and fireworks display. I'd been dreading it, fearing the inevitable collision of my at-home world and my hallowed Geek Camp existence. I could just imagine running into Sophie Allen, some tedious person like that, and she'd be all, *How's your summer? Have you started* Beowulf? *Did you hear about what happened last weekend at Jordan's house?* And then the veil would just come crashing down all over the place, and the spell—the incandescent bubble, the Grecian Urn, you get the point—would be broken. Louisville was the last place I wanted to go.

"I think we need a new plan."

Mason squinted in the sun. "What kind of plan?"

"I say we go rogue." On the surface of the pay phone, scrawled in what looked like lipstick, was yet another invitation to Call Ike for a Good Time.

"Put Cal on."

I held the receiver out to Calvin, who in turn proffered the blackberries. The corn was sunshine; the blackberry was summer itself, that singular achy sweetness. Later, when I would think back on this day—and I would, often—it would taste like Calvin's blackberries. Maybe it's ridiculous to pin a memory on a piece of fruit, but it was another thing I knew I wouldn't forget, ever.

"Do I have to talk on that germy phone?"

I shrugged and twirled the receiver around by its unwieldy cord. "We're concocting a plan. It seems an appropriate way to get the scheming done."

Cal played along, albeit reluctantly. "This phone smells like feet." He held the receiver a couple of inches away from his ear. "Calvin Little, at your service."

"Calvin. Bro. So how far away is this farm?"

13

Fireworks

BAMBOOZLING X was ridiculously, embarrassingly easy. I mean, I almost felt bad about it. Almost. We put Calvin in charge, since Cal had Holyfield on his side.

"X, this dog needs to run. When I took him out to the farm this morning, he went berserk. The farm sits on the highest point in Clark County—we'll get the best fireworks show around. Can't you exempt us from the field trip? Say it's class related?"

The catch was this: X and Kathryn and Juliet would be traveling with us. I balked at that arrangement until Mason pointed out the obvious, which was that we needed a ride. Kathryn deigned to risk her—and her offspring's—life in the Mystery Machine, and the whole unlikely lot of us arrived at Calvin's farm in time for supper. *Supper.* The very word felt like nourishment in my mouth. The sun was still high in the Fourth of July sky as we sat around this huge table—handmade of reclaimed barn wood by Cal's dad, who had also installed solar panels on the roof—and put away the most delicious meal I'd had in years: some kind of lasagna at the heart of which was something called Swiss chard—it was straight from the garden and, like the berries and the corn, seemed proof of the rightness of words like *wholesome* and *goodness,* words that TV commercials love but that usually don't apply to whatever they're trying to sell.

Chloe was right: Mr. and Mrs. Little—Jamison and Dot, they told us to call them—were awesome. The day was turning into a regular Mom Shopper's dream. Dot had this absentminded way of touching the back of Calvin's head whenever she passed him, and she called all of us "darlin'," as in *Chloe darlin', would you like some more sweet tea? So Mason darlin', Cal says you're an actor; is that right?* I couldn't decide which mom I loved more: Dot or Kathryn, whose new-mom fatigue seemed to have been replaced by a mysterious grace. Her hair was wound in a loose braid that trailed across her shoulder, and she seemed totally at ease there on the porch swing, laughing and talking, nursing Juliet beneath a baby blanket that appeared to be made from stitched-together pieces of neckties. Dot had produced the blanket from a trunk of things that used to belong to Calvin and Luke when they were babies.

"Far as I'm concerned, ties're for weddings and funerals, and still people want to give them at Christmas all the time," Jamison said. "Told Dot I didn't know what else to do with them, so when Luke came along she whipped a batch of the old ones into that baby blanket there."

"Cal and Luke both, back when they were babies, they used to love to rub that silk on their ears—helped them get to sleep," Dot said. "Lord, Calvin, you especially. You toted that thing around everywhere."

"Mom," Calvin protested.

Dot snapped out of her reverie and switched gears. "Now why don't yall take that dog outside and run him? Scoot, all yall. Daddy and I will tend to Mr. and Mrs. Xavier and this darlin' baby girl, bless her heart."

It was the only teeny thing I could hold against Dot—not a big deal, but still: I made a mental note to never, ever call my husband (assuming I one day had a husband, which maybe I wouldn't, whatever) *Daddy*. That right there is the kind of thing that can signal the beginning of the end, if you ask me.

"From the top of that hill, you can see for miles," Calvin said, leading the way. The sun hung low in the sky, drenching the treetops in its scarlet glow. We paused for a second to watch it take its slow-motion bow beneath the horizon: going, going, gone.

"Can't remember the last time I've seen that happen," Mason observed. "Where have I been?"

"Playing Street Fighter," Chloe said. "Hey. I brought stuff for s'mores."

"Up here's where we usually build the campfires," Calvin said. "Come on."

Calvin took off, Holyfield barking at his heels. Chloe followed them, laughing as she stretched both arms wide and pirouetted up the hill. Her raven hair against the slow melt of the sky, the pinwheel of her skirt as she spun: She looked like a bird taking flight. My mind snapped a picture of her, *click*.

I was taking my time getting up the hill. It'd been a while since I'd been surrounded by that much fresh air, that much wide-open beauty, and I felt a little unsteady, like I was treading within the fragile sphere of a dream. I had watched the sun blaze and in the blink of an eye slip away; the happiness I felt in that moment was a heartbeat from tipping to sadness at the knowledge that I couldn't hold it forever. My old familiar push-pull, my trademark yearning for and resisting joy.

"Hey Glo, come look at this."

Mason was twenty yards ahead of me, beckoning. I chose joy and let it propel me up the hill.

"There must have just been a hatch or something," Mason said. "Can you believe this?"

Blue butterflies. Hundreds of them, swooping about us in a frightening and gorgeous Hitchcock-esque swarm. They fluttered on the tall blades of grass, in Mason's hair, on his outstretched arms. He took my hand, and butterflies poured over my wrist. Their wings were startling and beautiful against my bare skin, and, maybe because in that moment I felt startling and beautiful by proxy, I pulled Mason to me and whispered in his ear, "Don't forget this."

As quickly as they had appeared, the butterflies swarmed away from us, all but one. It was perched on my shoulder, wings spread — waiting, I guess, to see how things would pan out. Mason made a move toward his camera, but I stopped him. "I've already got it," I said and, covering his hand with my own, I placed it over my heart. "I've got it right here."

Calvin got the fire going with expert Eagle Scout ease. Fireflies drifted up from the tall grass, rising as if to greet the fireworks that began, all at once, to burst in panoramic splendor all around us. We were so far away and so high up that the sound of the fireworks display never reached us. We were treated to an even more mysterious show: silent showers of red, white, and blue like paint slung on a canvas. Calvin lit sparklers for us, one by one. We wrote our names in the air, great sizzling swoops that left neon autographs behind our closed eyes.

"All right, Cal," Chloe said. "Give us the Declaration of Independence."

Calvin shook his head. "Can't do it on demand."

"Cal-vin," Chloe sang, "You know you know it."

Encircling the campfire were makeshift log benches; Calvin climbed atop the nearest one, closed his eyes, and pressed his right hand to his heart. He recited the whole thing—the absolute *entire* thing—with the same unexpected eloquence that he'd employed when he introduced us to *Nathan Coulter*. Goose bumps pricked up along my arms when he got to the part about *We hold these truths to be self-evident, that all men are created equal*. I mean, those are freaking goose-bump-inducing words right there. *Life, Liberty and the pursuit of Happiness*. I ask you: What else is there? It all seemed so simple and obvious and clear, and I wondered why the world couldn't just get with the program.

Chloe jumped to her feet and applauded. "That was awesome, Cal. Your brain astounds. But I still wish I lived in France."

"What's in France?" I asked. "I mean, besides the obvious."

"What's in Boone County?"

"Come on, it can't be that bad," I said. "High school's not forever. We're almost done."

"Easy for you to say," Chloe said, her voice rising. "I mean, you and Mason go to these performing-arts schools, right? Everybody accepts everybody and it's all *Glee* all the time."

"Don't even talk to me about *Glee*," Mason warned, "or I will be forced to vomit in your general direction."

"What I'm saying," Chloe went on, "is that it's okay to be different at your schools. In the cities where you live. I mean, it's more than okay. It's like *the* thing."

"Riiiight," Mason said. "And we're all so different that we're exactly the same." He punctuated this bit of wisdom by offering some exaggerated snoring sounds. Chloe stifled a laugh.

Here's the thing about my school: There are things I take for granted about it, maybe (such as: diversity and inclusion are so much a fact of life that words like *diversity* and *inclusion* aren't even necessary in every-day parlance), but it can still provide as hellish an environment as any other public high school in America. I still have to endure calculus and gym and Sophie Allen, whose reign as Head Princess has been in effect since kindergarten. That she's a future opera star with the voice of an angel doesn't make her any less of a pain in my ass.

"Chloe," I said, borrowing from Carol, "there are assholes everywhere you go. Even in Paris. *C'est la vie.*"

Mason crossed over to Calvin's log and sat down

211

beside him. He knocked gently on Cal's head. "What else have you got in there?"

Calvin looked up, as if the words could be found in the sky. "If more than used for brushing is accidentally swallowed, get medical help or contact a Poison Control Center right away."

Mason's eyes widened. "What the hell is that?"

Calvin shrugged. "Warning on the back of the toothpaste tube."

Chloe helped herself to a marshmallow. "I mean it, yall. What am I going to do without you?"

I had wondered the same thing myself, and hearing Chloe speak the words out loud brought a lump to my throat. In typical fashion I opted for funny. "Whatever! Aren't you sick of us yet?"

Chloe shook her head slowly back and forth. "Nope." She smiled at us, eyes glistening in the firelight. "I wish I could take all of you to school with me in the fall. Carry you in my pocket so I can remember what this feels like."

"What what feels like?" Mason asked.

"What it feels like to be myself," Chloe said.

Calvin reached for Chloe's bag and started rummaging around. "Any pen and paper in here?"

"Cal, I love you, but that's trespassing."

"Here we go." By the light of the fire Calvin started writing furiously with Chloe's oversized, fuzzy Hello Kitty pen.

"Should I even ask?" Mason said.

"I'm drawing up our contractual agreement," Calvin explained. "Gimme a second."

We watched, rapt, as Cal went into Thinking Mode. It was always fascinating to watch Calvin concentrate, but even better when his natural gravitas was juxtaposed against the goofy bobbing-along of a Hello Kitty pen.

"What kind of contract?" Mason asked.

"A friendship agreement," Calvin said. "To keep us in touch. Everybody has to abide by the terms."

Just the mention of it made me nervous. I knew I'd be bad at abiding by any terms, even if we made them up ourselves. As soon as I felt bound by something, it was my instinct to bail. Mason, in keeping with what had become an alarming pattern, yanked the words right from my head.

"No way, dude. I'm pleading Groucho Marx on this one. Yall're great and all, but I refuse to be a part of any club that would have me as a member. Don't let's get all clubby and sentimental."

Chloe pelted Mason with a marshmallow. "Whatever, Mr. Photography Club."

"That's different!"

"Different how?"

"That's *school*. What I do outside of school shouldn't involve contracts. Friendship, in general, shouldn't involve contracts."

I nodded in agreement.

Calvin frowned at the paper. "But man, this is good stuff."

"Here's what," Chloe said, rising to her feet. "I think a promise is a fabulous idea, but I respect that things like this make you, Mason, claustrophobic, and make you, oh worshipper of the Grecian Urn"—Chloe spun around and pointed at me—"uncomfortable as hell."

Mason and I exchanged a sheepish glance.

"But yall," Chloe went on, "I *need* you. I don't want to go back to Boone County in a few days and forget that any of this"—she swept her arms about, indicating the farm, the dark sky, the sparks rising like fairy dust from the fire—"ever happened. *Ça va?*"

Mason and I traded another glance. He nodded, just barely.

"Okay," I said. "Okay. First rule of the agreement: No social media?"

Chloe looked around at everyone. "Do we agree? Can everybody handle that?"

Three heads nodded. Holyfield snapped at a firefly.

"Do we want to say no e-mail or texts?" Calvin asked.

"I like it," Mason said. "Letters're what got us here in the first place."

"And we'll meet up at least, what, once every three months?" Chloe asked. "Quarterly?"

I cringed. "I think I feel a Grecian Urn moment coming on. Let's not push it."

"Okay okay," Chloe said. "Let's just plan our first rendezvous, sometime between, say, August and Christmas. Just something to look forward to so I won't die."

"We can meet at the Egg Drop and come back here," Calvin suggested. "In the fall, when the leaves change. Hayride, apples, harvest moon—"

"Somebody's birthday," Mason added airily.

I liked the leaves-and-apples scenario because it was in perfect alignment with my daydream. "That's good," I said. "Write that down, Cal."

"First day of fall?" Chloe suggested, face alight. "The equinox?"

"But my birthday's not until October!" Mason whined.

"Mason, God. Could you be a bigger baby? I'll bring cupcakes and we'll celebrate early. The equinox it is. Calvin, are you getting all this?"

Hello Kitty zoomed across the page.

Chloe was on a roll. "Make room for birthdays and addresses so that everybody gets plenty of love. If Mason gets cupcakes, we all get cupcakes."

"Who's gonna make your cupcakes?" Mason asked. "Because that's not really how I roll."

"I always accept fortune cookies and cards."

"But I don't send cards or—"

"Mason!" I screamed. "We get it. Chloe, I'll bake you some cupcakes."

We hovered over Cal's shoulder as he scrawled the final terms. "Okay," he said, wielding Hello Kitty like a wand. "Time to sign."

Calvin's contract was serious business, full of stuff like WHEREAS and WITNESSETH and *Now, therefore, in consideration of the above premises and the mutual promises, covenants, and terms contained herein.*

"What's with the jargon, Cal? Where'd you learn to write like this?"

"Eighth-grade mock trial. Back when everybody wanted to grow up to be president and save the world."

I entered my address and birthday and signed on the line. "Do we really need a notary?"

Calvin looked around. "Holyfield, come here. Chloe, can I borrow your lipstick?"

Chloe seemed to know what was coming next. "Dude, use a marker. Here."

Holyfield didn't object at all; he just lolled in Calvin's arms as Cal applied purple marker to the pads of his right front paw.

"Holyfield," he said, "you're as good a notary as any."

14

Stuff You Can't Put in a Letter

5 July

Dear Carol,

A Virginia Woolf garret!!! I like it! Can we afford it? Can we afford anything at all, anywhere? I kind of worry about how we're broke, how money doesn't grow on trees, etc., etc., etc. Anyway. I'm in but let's graduate first. You're right, I'm sentimental, getting more that way every second. For your eyes only, a list, if you will, of weird things about which I am currently sentimental:

1. Babies (!!!). Last night in X's bus I rode next to
baby Juliet. She was asleep in her carrier and in
the dark I held on to her little foot.
2. Taylor Swift songs. I know! Kill me now.
But dude, Taylor just pours out of the dorm
rooms all day long and I can't avoid it and
now I accidentally know all the words. Carol,
listen: That shit is poignant. I am not kidding.
Also, Taylor seems like a genuinely nice
person. Smart, too. I'm just saying. Do you
ever worry that our friendship is maybe based
on a shared disdain for too many people and
things? I propose we work on the Assholery.
Starting now.
3. The Mad Hatter. I know. Also an accident.
Obviously I need to get out of here before I lose
myself completely. I miss you. Almost as much as I
miss your mom, byotch. Next time you talk to her,
tell her hi from me.
Love,
Glo

I was hanging out in the laundry room, writing letters and listening to Alex's CD and enjoying the gentle
hypnosis provided by the spin of the dryer. The songs still
worked their magic on me, but Alex seemed far away,
much farther than Alaska.

5 July

Dear Alex,

Sorry it has taken me so long to write and thank you for the CD. I love it, I truly do. I hope things are going well in Talkeetna. I'm proud of you for going and hope I'll see you at Thanksgiving.

Love,
Gloria

It was the shortest, boringest, most unimaginative letter I'd ever written, but also the hardest and the most true. I was trying to work on saying what I meant and leaving it at that. Before I could change my mind—i.e., before I could embellish the letter with some of my trademark hyperbole—I sealed the envelope, addressed it, and affixed it with a stamp (Gregory Peck, of course. Atticus himself!).

Letter writing, I had discovered, was exhausting. Not just because of the effort of putting pen to paper, either. What I had written to Carol and Alex was one thing, but the mood of weird nostalgia that the act of writing put me in—well. That was quite another. There I was in the basement of Reynolds Hall, but my mind was back in sixth grade, Sunday mornings after sleepovers at Carol's house. Carol's mom always dragged everybody, including me, to church. I enjoyed the inevitable chaos of those mornings:

everybody bitching over the whine of the hair dryer, shoes and coats searched for and eventually found, Eggo waffles crammed into our mouths en route to the minivan. Carol and her brothers hated churchgoing on principle—the theft of their sleep, the uncomfortable clothes and forced niceties—but because I myself didn't go to church outside of these excursions (just another thing my parents couldn't agree on from the start), I came to the whole experience with a charged-up feeling that was half abject terror and half reverent curiosity.

First there was Sunday school. It made me uneasy because there I was, this weird girl wearing her best friend's clothes, an interloper among kids who had been going to church together since birth. It was sort of like being at the pool in the summer: There I'd be, all pale and freckled and clueless, flailing around in a pathetic attempt at a doggy paddle while all these other kids—born beneath the sea, apparently; born with gills and fins!—cut smooth, lithe paths through the pool and climbed out at the deep end, water gleaming on the sort of shoulder blades—tanned, angular—that could easily slice through melons.

So I was uneasy because of *that* whole load, but I was also uneasy because the Sunday school room smelled exactly like another basement room in another place in the back closet of my memory: Miss Lolly's preschool room, where my mother would drop off four-year-old me every day before going to work. I got a ridiculous amount of joy out of those drives from my house to preschool, if you want to know the truth. I would have my mother to myself for fifteen whole minutes, during which she would sing along with the radio—Celine Dion, Mariah Carey, horrible songs that nonetheless make me sob when I hear them in Muzak versions at the dentist's office—and I would listen to her voice and breathe in the familiar spicy scent of her perfume. Then we'd get to Miss Lolly's room and she would leave me. She'd leave me, and GoGo would pick me up. That's how it always went, right up until the day my mother left for good. GoGo picked me up that day, too, and kept picking me up—one school day, one piano lesson, one rehearsal, one orthodontist's appointment, one heartbreak or another at a time.

So. Apropos of what I was trying to get at: the Sunday school room in Carol's church smelled like Miss Lolly's preschool room, which is to say that it smelled like Leaving. I liked it better when we went upstairs to the Big Church, where it smelled like Incense and Mystery. For Carol and her brothers, this part was torture of the utmost (Carol would zone out during the sermon and write me notes on the program—*That guy is picking his nose!*, etc., etc.). As for me, I was so ashamed of and bewildered by my own church ineptitude—not to mention agonized by Carol's too-small-for-me, itchy clothes—that most of what transpired was completely lost on me. People would keep standing up and sitting back down and kneeling and

221

saying stuff in eerie unison, and I would just feel like disappearing. There was this one part of the liturgy, though, that I truly loved and looked forward to every time. It happened just before the Communion, when the choir would sing this song with a bunch of hallelujahs in it. That part, man—that was something special. I could cry just thinking about it, and I did, out of nowhere as I was writing that über-boring letter to Alex. Those voices, rising up to greet the ceiling? They were *it*. Bound up in those voices was the same magic, the same mystery, that I felt under the stars at Calvin's farm. The same wonder I felt when Mason was standing before me, wearing a sleeve of butterflies. I felt it again in the Mystery Machine as I held baby Juliet's tiny foot in my hand. That behold-the-ocean feeling. That kiss-a-boy feeling, times ten.

Anyway. Carol's mom quit forcing her kids to go to church once they got to high school. I never went back, either, but those voices of the choir have stayed with me. I was tempted to share that with Carol and Alex in my letters, but instead I stuck with what I was trying to say. The beginning of it, anyway. What was the rest of what I was trying to say? That I love you? That being a small part of your family has been the best gift of my life, that it has provided me with more joy and proof of God than any rocker-slash-evangelist in a pair of jeans could ever in a million years give me? Dear Alex: That kiss was awesome and the CD rocks and I love to fall asleep thinking about your eyelashes, but your mom's the one I'm really in love with and can I please have her, please and thank you, please?

Yeah, something like that. But that's not really the kind of stuff you can put in a letter unless you want somebody to think you've gone completely batshit-crazy with a cherry on top.

So I was balancing the laundry basket on my hip and digging around in my pocket for my room key when I heard voices. On the other side of the door to room 317, Jessica and Sonya were singing. Some kind of duet, and Sonya was doing the low part.

"Shit," came Sonya's voice, breaking apart from the song. "Can we start again?"

As quietly as I could, I lowered the laundry to the floor and propped myself against the door. The hallway was empty; I had this show to myself.

"Want me to do alto?" Jess asked.

"No, you're better on soprano. I got it, I got it. Let's just start again."

I could picture them in there, closing their eyes and letting their voices braid together. The song was something I'd never heard before, something about Gloaming and My Darling and the Lights, Soft and Low. My friends' voices were surprisingly lovely; if I hadn't known it was Jessica and Sonya in there, I never would have guessed that the voices could belong to them.

For my heart was tossed with longing . . .

Tossed with longing. The story of my life, maybe?

It was best to leave you thus, dear, best for you and best for me . . .

The song was sad as hell! Where had they gotten hold of this sad song? Their voices trailed off and, after a moment of quiet (another iridescent bubble; I held my breath), they both burst out laughing.

"Did I get it that time?" Sonya asked.

"You nailed it, girl."

"Are we talent-show ready?"

"As ready as we're gonna be."

More laughter, and they launched into a rousing duet version of one of those Taylor Swift songs that for days had been cruising around uninvited in my head. I reached for the knob and then thought better of it. I waited until they finished the song, then I hefted my laundry and headed back down the stairs.

15

Borboleta

IT WAS our third week at geek camp, and Chloe had requested of X that she be permitted to present her Great American Novel at the Egg Drop. Xiu Li had agreed to open a half hour early on Chloe's behalf; this meant that we all had to get up way early, so everyone was grumpy. Mason gulped coffee and Calvin tapped the window, on the other side of which was Holyfield, looking forlorn.

"I'll bring you some scrambled eggs, buddy, don't worry."

"Calvin, you shouldn't baby that dog so much," X said. "So are we all met? Are we ready to get this show on the road?"

"Almost ready!" Xiu Li announced. She was clad in one of Chloe's flapper dresses and was carrying a tray full of little glasses of something frothy and pink. "Sloe gin fizzes!"

Calvin was aghast. "Xiu Li, it is seven thirty in the morning. I'm seventeen."

Xiu Li couldn't have looked more pleased. She set the tray on the table and clapped her hands. "Drink up!"

Some kind of swanky speakeasy music started pouring out of the jukebox, and Chloe emerged from the swinging kitchen doors, swishy in her own fringed dress. She had a long string of beads around her neck and was smoking an unlit cigarette stuck onto the end of an elegant holder. I could see why Chloe fancied this era so much; she so looked the part. I exchanged grins with Calvin and Mason and we settled in for what promised to be an entertaining show.

A moment later the kitchen doors swung open again and another unexpected player emerged on the scene: the beautiful Latina girl from down the hall. She had been catching my eye since Geek Camp began, but I'd been too intimidated to approach her — she seemed years older than everyone else, oozing experience and sophistication in her pointy boots, dark eyeliner, and bright, tight clothes. She was the kind of girl who seemed in possession of the *facts,* is what I'm saying. One morning on the way to the shower

I caught a glimpse of her in her room, kneeling before a silk-draped altar of candles and a miniature version of that ginormous Jesus statue in Brazil. *Christ the Redeemer, one of the new seven wonders of the world,* I remember thinking stupidly as I stood there, too spellbound to know I was staring. She had looked up then and smiled at me, a kind smile that said *come in,* but I'd beelined for the bathroom, horrified at having been caught gawking. Now she was standing before me in a flapper dress, swinging a tennis racket, her dark hair wound around her head in a thick rope.

"This is Jimena," Chloe announced. "She's Jordan Baker. I'm Daisy, obviously."

Jimena waved. "*Olá,* yall."

Chloe looked at Jimena. "Ready?"

Jimena nodded. "*Sim.*"

Chloe put on a bored expression and draped herself in the nearest booth. She gazed at her audience with impressive Daisy-esque languor. "'In two weeks it'll be the longest day of the year,'" she drawled. "'Do you always watch for the longest day of the year and then miss it? I always watch for the longest day in the year and then miss it.'"

On cue, Jimena threw her arm across her forehead as if she too were very, very bored. She yawned ostentatiously. "We ought to plan something."

Chloe/Daisy perked up and rose from the booth. "All right. What'll we plan?" She ran to Calvin and flung her arms around him. "What do people plan?"

Calvin looked around, panicked. "Am I supposed to say something? Because I do not have *Gatsby* memorized, if that's what you're thinking. You can't just expect me to—"

"Shhhh!" Chloe ordered. She detached herself from Calvin and stepped back to where Jimena was standing. They gripped hands and bowed. Xiu Li commenced vigorous applause.

X raised his eyebrows. "Is that it?"

Chloe's shoulders dropped. "What do you mean, is that it? Of course that's it. That's my favorite part of the book. You've just witnessed a dramatic interpretation of my favorite part of the book, X, hello."

"Ahhhhh," X said, backpedaling. "Gotcha, gotcha." He looked around at us and nodded. "So. Can you tell us why it's your favorite part?"

Chloe and Jimena exchanged a confused glance.

"Because," Chloe said. "Because to me, that's what the whole book is about. You wait and wait for something wonderful to happen and then it happens when you're not looking. Either that or it doesn't happen at all."

This was a thing I understood, not just a little bit but a huge, fiery lot. I was about to voice my understanding when Chloe started to cry. Mason grabbed a handful of

228

napkins and rose from his seat to offer them to her. Before, I would have scoffed at that move—here's the Mad Hatter, using Chloe's frustration as a chance to call attention to himself—but now I saw the gesture for what it was: Mason being nice. He could be really nice, really thoughtful, when he wanted to be.

"Forget it," Chloe said, blowing her nose. She yanked the spangly feathered band from her head and tossed it on a table. "This is stupid. It's too hard to explain. I can't say why I love the book. I just do. You don't pick the books you fall in love with any more than you pick the people you fall in love with. It just happens, and when it happens, you know. Who's to say where love comes from?"

Chloe shifted her wet gaze briefly to Jimena, whose face appeared lit from within. The joy was contagious, like when a person yawns: I looked around at my friends and we were all wearing ridiculous grins.

Chloe grabbed one of Xiu Li's sloe gin fizzes, sank into the booth beside me, and started gulping. "This is awesome, Xiu Li. Thank you."

Xiu Li tipped her head in a compassionate nod. I took one of the glasses and clinked it against Chloe's. "I thought you were great." Then, I couldn't resist a whispered dig: "Girl, you've been holding out on us!"

Chloe shrugged, grinning hugely. "It happened when I wasn't looking."

"X," Chloe said, shifting gears. "This is hard. I really did want to get it right. I'm sorry if I let you down."

"You didn't let me down," X said. "In fact, you illustrated the point beautifully. You gave me exactly what I asked for."

"Failure?"

"Passion."

Chloe managed a smile. "Yeah, well. Passion's not going to get me into the Sorbonne."

X shrugged. "Who says? You might be surprised. I hear the French are big on passion."

Chloe smiled all the way. *"Oui oui."*

"Now," X continued, "one more sip and then yall need to stop imbibing. My job is on the line. Thank you, Xiu Li, for the drinks and the atmosphere. This has been smashing. Are we ready to head to class? It's time for a little James Joyce, people."

The air was electric with the promise of rain. Not just rain but a storm—the kind you can smell drifting toward you on the breeze. GoGo had taught me that if you can see the undersides of the leaves, a storm is coming. Holyfield sensed it, too—he led the way to class with his ears lifted and a tiny Mohawk raised on his back.

Halfway to the classroom building, Chloe paused to say goodbye to Jimena. They'd been holding hands as they walked and now they were wrapped in a long embrace — long for eight in the morning, anyway.

"Don't *stare*," I said to Calvin, whacking his arm.

"I'm not staring!"

I steered Calvin onward and grabbed Mason's sleeve with my free arm. "Give them a little privacy, yall, come on."

We were hunching forward against the quickening wind when Jimena called out to us. "It was very nice to meet all of you!"

I stopped and turned, yanking Calvin and Mason around with me. "It was nice to meet you, too, Jimena. You're a great Jordan Baker."

Jimena raised her arm and pointed. A blue butterfly was flying toward her, beating its wings against the wind. "They'll be gone after this storm. This one's stopping to say goodbye."

"She knows about this stuff," Chloe said to us. Then, leaning into Jimena, "Hey, tell them about the legends."

Jimena blushed. Her hair was whipping about her face; she unwound a strand from her neck and pulled another away from her mouth. "No, no. It's silly."

"It's not silly!" Chloe protested. "Gloria, you'll love this. So, where Jimena comes from, these butterflies are a very big deal. Some people think they're evil — like tricksters or something, like in fables — "

"That's not what I think, though," Jimena added. "I think they're good luck. My *avó* always said that every *borboleta* is the soul of a dead loved one, coming back to make peace or to watch over the living."

"Really?" Mason asked. His eyes were following the butterfly as it swooped around Holyfield's head. I wondered what he was thinking, or if he was wondering what I was thinking.

"I like that better than the evil thing, even though I think they are kind of scary," Calvin said. "I mean, they've got global warming written all over them, don't you think?"

I squinted against the wind, which was getting a little bizarre itself. "What'd you say the life span is, Cal?"

"One hundred and fifteen days."

"I'm telling you, this storm is day one hundred fifteen for them. Just watch," Jimena said.

I stared at the butterfly — *borboleta, mariposa, papilio,* the thing is beautiful in every language — and as if I had willed it toward me by some one-time-only kind of telekinesis, it fluttered right into my outstretched palm. *GoGo,* I thought. *Is that you?*

It rose into the air and disappeared. Jimena was right: The storm rolled in like a freight train, and after that the butterflies disappeared like a dream washed away by daylight.

If you had told me a story about those butterflies,

about all the strange and marvelous ways they made my life magic that summer, I'd have said that you were crazy. I'd have said that you were a little bit drunk on metaphor, or that Nabokov had gone to your head, or that you must have just *imagined* all those butterflies, you with your penchant for hyperbole, because come on, dude, how many South American blue butterflies can you cram into one stupid story?

Yeah, well. Truth is stranger than fiction, people. I'm telling you: The butterflies came, and they were magic, and then they were gone. The magic, though? The magic is what stayed.

16

Magically Delicious

Dear Glo,

　　Greetings from scenic North Bergen, New Jersey, home of the closest Dairy Queen to New York City. I took the TRAIN. That is how much I am STARVING. That is how much I MISS YOU. I'm off to find a stamp to put on this thing.

　　Love,
　　Carol

P.S. Oscar came to visit over the weekend. Something BIG happened. That is your only hint! Stay tuned for details . . .

I was getting that scowly, panicky feeling of having missed something. I knew exactly what Carol's Something Big was, and I couldn't believe she would allow it to happen in another *state,* when I wasn't even around! Not that she needed my permission, not that I wanted to be in the same room with her or anything, but still. I felt bereft. Left behind. Stranded in kindergarten with the virgins and the finger-painters. And Chloe! Where had she found the time and space to fall in love? I'd been at Geek Camp all that time but had only just met Jimena. How many other fascinating people had I missed? Why hadn't I made half an effort? Where had I been? What, exactly, had I been doing? GoGo would have kicked my ass: *Don't be so* insular, *sweetheart,* she used to tell me. *Don't be so bitter and standoffish! People are one of life's greatest joys; make an effort to know them and get along with as many different kinds of people as you can.* In general I tried to live up to GoGo's advice, I really did, but it was hard. Inevitably, people would get on my nerves. *Maybe,* I thought with horror, *maybe* you *get on people's nerves, Gloria Aaron Bishop.*

Even Calvin was acting weird: At breakfast I'd seen him eating with this girl—an unabashedly gorgeous girl, one of the Modern Dancers. She was wearing actual leg warmers and was throwing back her head and laughing like Calvin was just the funniest person ever to land on the planet. I was crossing the room to join them, my tray wobbly with milk and juice and Lucky Charms, when Calvin shot me this embarrassed, apologetic, positively whiplashed-by-love look: *Not now,* the look said. *I'll explain later.* I could tell Calvin had it bad because he was rubbing his left leg with his right foot in that way he does when he's nervous. Unbelievable. Calvin Little was wooing a Modern Dancer! The Calvinisms just went on and on.

I parked my tray at an empty corner table and was fixing to drown myself in Lucky Charms and my sorrows when Mason appeared out of (as usual!) nowhere. I was so happy to see him that I decided to cut the bullshit for just one second and actually tell him I was happy to see him.

"Really?" he asked.

"Yes," I said. "Don't ruin it."

We smiled at each other for a second. It was a delicious second, I have to say.

"We need one more rehearsal," Mason said, suddenly all business. "Check it out."

He held out his palm, on which rested a slender silver key.

"What's that?"

"The key to McGrath's tomb."

My mind did some quick, suspicious arithmetic. "So have you and Meghan rekindled your romance?"

"No. Which is why I have zero qualms about stealing stuff from her desk. Are you done eating or what?"

⌒

McGrath's tomb looked completely different this time around. Smaller, somehow. Darker. More mysterious.

"What if there's a tour?"

Mason shrugged. "We'll cross that bridge if we get there."

"What if we get caught?"

"Caught doing what? We're rehearsing for a freaking talent show."

"Caught trespassing. Caught stealing keys. You know, property of Morlan College?"

Mason looked exasperated. "Are you seriously this big of a groundbird? I'm shocked, Gloria Bishop."

"Groundbird? What?"

Mason hoisted himself up onto McGrath's stone slab. "Gloria. I will pay you to stop sabotaging everything. Will you just get up here, please?"

Mason was not the first to accuse me of blowing fantastic moments when they had the good grace to come around. Carol says I'm famous for it: I go around wishing for things to happen and then as soon as they start happening I go into Sabotage Mode.

"Fine." I climbed up.

"Let's just do a quick read-through."

"Okay."

"Here," Mason said. "Turn around."

I turned and Mason twisted his body so that we were sitting back to back. He linked elbows with mine.

"What are you doing?"

"Shhh," Mason said. "Start when you're ready."

I took a deep breath and stared at the wall in front of me. There was the drawing of the chalk girl, staring right back at me. *Go on*, she seemed to say.

I leaned my head back against Mason's shoulder. He smelled like his soapy self. God. I had to take another breath so I could get it together.

"'I wonder that you will still be talking, Signor Benedick. Nobody marks you.'"

Mason sat up straighter, dislodging my head.

"'What, my dear Lady Disdain! Are you yet living?'"

I could feel each bone of Mason's spine against my own. I was totally discombobulated. The next line seemed to hover in the air before me, then I lost it. I closed my eyes and looked for it, like I was doing the Jumble. Nothing was behind my eyes but Mason's face, his detestable, irresistible grin. When I opened my eyes, the chalk girl seemed to be whispering to me; the line came flying back to my tongue.

"'Is it possible disdain should die while she hath such meet food to feed it as Signor Benedick? Courtesy itself must convert to disdain if you come in her presence.'"

We bounced the lines back and forth, our voices answering each other like the sharp-edged, trained instruments they were. Neither one of us faltered. We had it down, this business of highbrow witty banter. We were pros!

"It seems really short," Mason said when we'd run through the whole thing. "Should we get Kyle to read Don Pedro and Leonato?"

We were still back to back, and we leaned these questions into each other's ears.

"Who's Kyle?"

"My roommate. Kyle, aka Edward Softly. Although last week he had a change of heart and is now calling himself d'Artagnan."

"Can d'Artagnan be trusted to handle this?"

Mason thought about it for a second. "No."

"Okay then," I said. "We're on our own. It'll be short but sweet."

A silence settled over us, during which I became aware that our breathing was taking on the same rhythm.

"You know all that stuff I told you?" Mason asked. "That stuff about my dad?"

I nodded against his head.

"Well it's not like I just go around telling everybody that stuff. Just so you know."

I nodded again. Our hair was tangled together in this staticky mat.

"It's not your fault, you know," I whispered.

"Say it again."

"It's not your fault."

"Louder."

"It's not your fault!" I yelled. The tomb seemed to trap my voice in the cool of its walls; I had a feeling that we could scream our heads off all day long and our voices would never leave the room.

"That was loud," Mason laughed. "It's also something—the *one* thing—I've wanted to hear for years. It sounds good."

"My turn," I said. I shifted, tightened my elbow grip, and held on. "I want to hear what it sounds like, too."

Mason turned his head so that I could feel his breath curl into my ear. His eyes were closed. "It's not your fault," he whispered.

He said it again. And again. And I said it with him, over and over, louder and louder until we were hoarse, until we were screaming with laughter, tears of joy and rage filling our eyes. My arms ached from holding on so tight; my throat burned. I felt a thousand pounds lighter; I could have easily wisped into the air and floated through the keyhole.

"Man," I said, lolling my head against Mason's. "Beatrice and Benedick. They are so full of shit."

Mason's body seemed to slacken. I thought he might be falling asleep until he gave my left elbow a gentle tug.

"So what do you think of my artwork?" he asked.

The chalk girl grinned at me. She might have even winked. *I've got your number, girl.*

"Wait a minute."

"A pretty good rendering, if I do say so myself."

"I thought you were claustrophobic."

"Well, I couldn't have you thinking I'd been down here before, now, could I? Anyway, I am claustrophobic. It was not fun to be in this place by myself."

The weird thing about the chalk girl was that it wasn't so much the shape of her features that looked like me; it was her expression. It was some nameless thing happening in her face—something that seemed to change each time I looked at her.

"Huh," I said, not getting anywhere near what I wanted to say.

"That's you in the window," Mason said, whispering again. "On that first day. Remember? You were up there all bright-angel Juliet-like, and I was just minding my own business, and you looked at me like you hated my guts. It was hate at first sight. How could I resist?"

I studied the chalk girl again. She didn't look like she hated anybody. She looked the way I felt: knocked right out of her senses by a feeling so huge and foreign and dis-orienting and straight-out-of-nowhere that it had to be something like love.

241

17

Curtain Call

"THE GREAT AMERICAN Novel hasn't been written yet," Mason declared. Rain streaked along the windows of the classroom building, and the overhead lights buzzed and flickered ominously. Holyfield curled himself beneath Calvin's desk and whimpered. It was our last class, and the mood was one of impending gloom-doom.

"Either that," Mason continued, "or it's hidden beneath the floorboards somewhere in J. D. Salinger's house."

The rain graduated to hail. A yellow puddle appeared beneath Holyfield's shaking haunches.

"Just one sec," Calvin said, quietly excusing himself from the room.

Chloe took a long drag on her pencil. "Or maybe," she said, "maybe it's been written but you just haven't *read* it yet."

Mason shook his head. "Impossible."

God. Every time I was tempted to fall for Mason Atkinson, he had to go and remind me of why I hated his guts in the first place.

Then he looked right at me and winked. "Just kidding."

I tried not to smile, but it was useless. Even the roots of my hair were smiling.

X sighed. "Thank you, Mason. That was certainly illuminating."

Calvin returned with a clutch of paper towels. "What'd I miss?"

"Nothing," Chloe said. She gathered Holyfield into her arms. "Gloria, you're on."

Here it was: the moment I'd been dreading. I clutched GoGo's book in my hand and crossed to the front of the room. As I stood there, looking at X and my friends and Holyfield, it occurred to me that I wasn't cut out for this at all. Getting up on a stage and spouting Shakespeare was one thing, but standing up in front of people and being me, Gloria Aaron Bishop, and talking about something that's so dear to me I just don't even know what? That was quite another.

"So," I said, trying to be casual. I waved the book around. "*To Kill a Mockingbird.*"

Already the lump was rising in my throat. Already the tears were gathering behind my eyes. This was what I had feared: that I wouldn't be able do it. I looked at Chloe and she nodded, her eyes huge and warm. It occurred to me then that I loved her, that she was a truly good person and an excellent friend, that I was lucky, lucky to know her. There was Calvin, next to her: Calvin Little, Lepidopterist and Mad-Farmer-in-Training. He smiled at me in a way I hoped I deserved, because that's how it is with Calvin—when you're around him you want to have *earned* his trademark respect and integrity. You want to rise to the occasion. There was X, waiting. I had been hard on him; I had suspected him of the same disease that plagued so many of my teachers at school—general burnout, or a general self-indulgent unwillingness to grow up long enough to be a role model for somebody else. The truth was that he had trusted us, he had been *earnest* with us, and that I wouldn't forget him anytime soon. And Mason? I couldn't look at him. If I looked at him I knew I wouldn't be able to speak at all.

I looked right at Holyfield and said, "I love this book because of the father in it. There aren't many books with really memorable fathers, and this one, at least I think, is the best."

My dad rose up in my mind, a scene from years ago: He was wearing this goggle-magnifying-glass thing on his head and he was ordering me to *sit still* while he patiently combed again and again through every strand of my splendid waist-length hair while I cried, full-on snot-cried, like my life was coming to end. My life wasn't coming to an end, of course, but I did have a raging case of head lice, and any other single father of an eight-year-old girl would have just hacked off all that hair, would have just gotten rid of it instead of spending hours making sure that every nit and egg was gone from what his daughter was convinced was her one single beauty—her hair was her glory and her security blanket, and to lose it would have broken her heart. My father. My very own modern-day Atticus Finch. He has eradicated head lice in the middle of the night. He has collected pads and tampons from the twenty-four-hour drugstore, has spent hundreds of dollars replacing retainers and other orthodontic paraphernalia lost forever to the depths of school cafeteria trash cans, has seen me heartbroken, really heartbroken, and has held me tight as I cried. He has done these and a million other things that people mistakenly believe to be the responsibility of mothers, when in truth sometimes fathers are the very best people for the job.

"Also," I managed to say, "also I love this book because it was my grandmother's favorite, and she read it to me out loud when I was younger"—here I thought for sure the tears were going to give up and spill; I wanted so badly to just finish what I had to say, to get it right just this once—"and to me it's *her*, it's her voice. I guess what I'm trying to say is that sometimes you can love a book not so much because of what it's about or what happens in it, but because it belongs to a certain time or person in your life—like you'll always remember where you were when you read it for the first time, or who gave it to you, or what season it was, or who you were before you read it and how you were different when it was over."

I swallowed. So far the tears had stayed put.

"I don't know if that makes any sense, but that's it. That's why I love this book."

"That, and Boo Radley."

At the sound of Mason's voice my eyes flicked up and met his for the first and only time since I'd been standing there, shaking in my boots.

"Yeah," I said. "And Boo Radley."

The lights were still doing their weird disco-flicker.

X started to clap. He rose from his seat, still clapping, and stood before us.

"Bravo, yall. Give yourselves a round of applause. This has been a great class."

We looked at each other nervously. It felt too ridiculous to clap along with X, and it was our duty to sort of look at one another and then at him like, *Yeah, how lame is that, how big of a dork is he,* but the truth is that we knew, each of us, that our summer together could have

been a lot worse, and that maybe it had even been wonderful, and that we weren't in any huge hurry for it to
come to an end.

I sat in the very last seat on the bus. Jessica and Sonya
sat in front of me, practicing their heartbreaking song for
the talent show that night. It was even more heartbreaking
in the rain, which was still pouring down by the bucket-
ful. In the gloom the lush lawns of the horse farms really
did look sort of blue. *Oh, my gorgeous Bluegrass State*,
I thought. *Where have you been all my life?* Bluegrass
State: We had learned the nickname in elementary school,
along with Cardinal, Coffee Tree, and "My Old Kentucky
Home." We had learned to find our state on the map, and
ever since then—even now—any time I look at any map
of the United States, my eyes go straight to our little race-
car–shaped state, right at the place where the country's
heart would be if it placed its hand across its chest to say
the Pledge of Allegiance. It's weird, the bizarre thoughts
that go through your head when you're riding in the back
of a school bus in the rain. I was getting carried away. No
doubt the eyes of people from Colorado go straight to that
clean rectangle, to that perfect right-angle crossroads with
its postage-stamp neighbors; Oklahomans' eyes go straight
to their tipped-over foam finger (Go, Sooners!), pointing
thataway. You learn to see things a certain way and it's
hard to change your perspective, is what I'm saying.

"Glo, are you awake?" Jessica hung over the back of her seat. "How'd we sound?"

I tried to pull myself out of my daze. "Y'all sound awesome."

Jessica hovered there for a second, assessing my mood. "Are you okay?"

"I'm fine," I said. "I'm good."

She reached out and picked up a strand of my hair. "Are you going to let us fix you up tonight?"

I smiled. I'd never have admitted it, but I was going to miss our Makeover Nights. "Okay. But I don't want all that black stuff on my eyes."

Jessica twirled my hair around her finger and grinned. "Your Mad Hatter won't know what hit him."

Brayden was the first kid to meet us at the door of the three-year-old room. She had on a fire helmet and was carrying a makeshift hose.

"Miss Gloria!"

I'd been hoping she would remember me, and when she did I couldn't help it: I opened my arms and gave her a hug, the biggest I could manage.

"Are you going to read to us today?"

I exchanged a glance with Sonya, who tipped a book into my hand.

"Yeah," I said. "It's my turn to read."

I didn't expect them to listen, but they did. As I read

from this book about a fireman and his dog, the kids all just looked up at me, hanging on my words, like, *Man, it just doesn't get any better than this.* There were maybe seven or eight of them, and I tried hard to look at all of their faces, to match their faces with their names so that I'd remember them. Somebody had dropped each one of them off that morning—they'd come into this room straight out of the facts of their own lives—and somebody would pick them up at the end of the day. Sometimes they played with clay and sometimes they got to swing on the swings and on some days, days like this one, new people—foreign ambassadors from the Big World Out There!—would show up out of the blue and read books about firefighters or police dogs or caterpillars or princesses or whatever. They wouldn't remember a lot of it, but some of it, *some of it*—the way the room smelled, say, or the fire drill they would have in an hour—would stay with them all their lives.

After the End-of-Geek-Camp banquet (we all got dressed up; there was frighteningly overdone roast beef and a sheet cake the size of a car), everybody filed into the auditorium for the talent show. I hadn't seen Mason anywhere and I was starting to worry that he had changed his mind.

"You look really pretty," Chloe said. "I like the hair!"

I put a hand to my head, which Jessica and Sonya had

worked on for an hour. They had ironed my hair into a long ponytail with braids wrapped around the top. I felt very Greek Goddess-y, very Grey-Eyed-Athena-y, in my talent show getup.

"Thanks," I said. "So do you."

Chloe and Jimena both had flowers in their hair; Jimena reached up and took one from her own loose bun. "Here," she said, fitting it into the side of my ponytail. "Now you're perfect."

"Wait," Chloe said. "One more thing." She reached into her bag and came up with a jack-o'-lantern Pez dispenser. "Everybody needs Pez for luck."

Jimena and Chloe and I chewed our candy and hugged one another. Just as the house lights were dimming (there is nothing like the hush and thrill of a darkening theater, nothing in this world) and Tweed was approaching his old friend the Podium, Calvin and his dancer friend—her name was Hayley, Chloe whispered to me with no small amount of glee—came in, closely followed by X and then Xiu Li, who waved wildly when she caught sight of Chloe and me. Together, we all slid into a row near the front. I kept the seat to my left—the one on the aisle—empty and prayed that Mason would show up. Chloe was on my right; she squeezed my hand as Tweed tapped on the microphone.

"Can yall hear me in the back?"

A paper airplane came sailing across everybody's

heads and landed gently at Tweed's feet. I craned around and there was Mason, draped across two seats in the back row. I tried to shoot him a death-glare, but all I had for him was a huge, relieved, involuntary smile. I mouthed *Get down here!* and beckoned furiously.

"I'll take that as a yes," Tweed continued. He cleared his throat, straightened his back, and launched into what was apparently some sort of prepared speech.

"Abraham Lincoln," he said.

Dramatic pause.

"Muhammad Ali."

Another weighty pause.

"Henry Clay. Simon Kenton. George Clooney. Diane Sawyer. Johnny Depp and his inimitable muse, Mr. Hunter S. Thompson."

Chloe and I slid a glance at each other. We'd heard this roll call before. Yes, it was nice that all these cool people were from Kentucky, but the things they have in common—

"What do all these folks have in common?" Tweed asked, all puffed up with civic and academic pride.

—the things they have in *common* are (a) they're famous, which is fantastic and all, as long as you're willing to buy into the notion that to be a worthwhile person you must also be a *famous* person; and (b) hello, they no longer live in Kentucky and probably couldn't wait to bail in the first place; and (c) there are interesting people from everywhere. Every state has its own freaking impressive-native roll call. Come on, people.

"They're all native Kentuckians," Tweed concluded, in case he thought we'd been lobotomized. "They're all ambassadors of our own Bluegrass State. They've all done our state proud and have paved the way for each of *you*"—Tweed indicated all 120 of us with a grand sweep of his arm—"to do great things yourselves. As graduating members of the Commonwealth Summer Program for Gifted and Talented Students, each of you has earned not only the promise of success, but also a full scholarship to Kentucky's own flagship university—in our eyes, that's testament to our investment in your bright future. We hope you'll stick around to keep making your state great. It's up to you whether or not you choose to become the next Robert Penn Warren."

Dramatic pause.

"The next Gus Van Sant."

Mason slid into the seat next to me and squeezed my knee.

Tweed was just settling into his next Dramatic Pause when Mason cupped his hands around his mouth and shouted up at him, "Don't forget Richard Hell!"

"Right *on*," Chloe said. She reached across me and gave Mason a high-five.

"Tom Cruise went to high school with my uncle!" someone shouted from the back.

"Ashley Judd!" somebody else screamed.

"That hot chick from *Dexter*!" came another voice, and somebody whistled in agreement.

"Michael Shannon!"

"My papaw!"

"Calvin's mom!" I hollered, and Calvin touched his forehead at me in salute.

The room had turned into a chorus of people calling out names and laughing. Apparently half of all Geek Campers had at one point gone to school with, ridden in a car alongside, or encountered at the gas station the one and only Jennifer Lawrence. Tweed held up his hands in an effort to corral the chaos.

"All right, all right, proud Kentuckians. Thank you for a great summer. Now, without further ado, I'm pleased to introduce our first talented talent show participants, Sonya Henderson and Jessica Dixon."

To the accompaniment of wild applause, Sonya and Jess took the stage. It was the first time I had ever seen Sonya look nervous, and her nervousness made her look even more beautiful than usual. Jessica spotted me in the audience and waved. I waved back and clapped as hard as I could, and I couldn't stop smiling, so much smiling that my face ached and my eyes got all swimmy. God, Geek Camp had turned me into such a *crier*. My friends sang their beautiful, sad song and didn't miss a note. When they clasped hands and took a shared bow, everybody roared.

I was so proud of them I thought my heart would burst from my chest. Never, not ever in a million years, would I have guessed myself to be the sort of person who would get all emotionally turned upside down by a high-school talent show, but there it was.

"How'd we do?" Jess asked breathlessly. She and Sonya fell into two seats in the row in front of us. I reached over and hugged Jess—she had taught me the art of hugging, after all—and told her that she was wonderful, that I was going to miss her, that so many people had said my hair looked pretty. She slid her eyes in Mason's direction and raised her eyebrows in approval. I shushed her and sank back into my seat as the lights dimmed for the next act.

The boy who made his quiet way to center stage was someone I recognized from my own school—a small kid, nimble, part of the math and science magnet program, which is basically no-man's-land if you're part of the Performing Arts School. His name was Darren something. I didn't really know him from school and had hardly seen him at all around Geek Camp. All over again I felt that grasping sense of loss, like I had spent four precious weeks with my head in the sand. I felt a sudden fierce devotion to every single Geek Camper in the room; I wanted to start over at the beginning and have at least one meaningful conversation with each of them.

Darren something, it turns out, knew how to robot like you wouldn't believe. Before our eyes, his body morphed into something mesmerizing and impossible. Everybody went wild, rising to their feet and screaming with appreciation. Then Darren swung his arms together, clapping a strong and steady beat. When he had the whole audience in his thrall, clapping along with him, he started rapping. This tiny little math-and-science white kid, killing the shit out of this rap he had obviously made up right there on the spot:

Dear Muhammad Ali
Oh, say can you see?
Come back to River City
And fix it for me.
Dear Johnny Depp
Mr. Ken-tuck-y
You saved the West Memphis Three
But what about me?
Dear George Clooney
You got what it takes
How 'bout uppin the stakes
Lead these You-Knighted States . . .

After that I couldn't even hear what Darren was riffing, the applause was so uproarious. I had visions of

George Clooney actually running for president and taking Darren Something along on the campaign trail. Darren was going to be a tough act to follow, and Mason and I were next.

"Nervous?" Mason asked.

I nodded.

"Good," he said, and took my hand. "I'd be nervous if you weren't nervous."

I closed my eyes for just a second to enjoy the feeling of having my hand in Mason's hand. It occurred to me that I was way past pretending that it wasn't my new favorite feeling in the world.

Chloe nudged me with her elbow.

"Finally," she whispered.

Finally.

The lights dimmed as Darren disappeared into the wings.

Mason rose from his seat and, heart pounding, I followed him. In the half-dark, as the chatter of our friends settled down around us, we walked together until we reached the stage. Mason pushed himself up and pulled me up after him.

There we were, in our pool of light.

"'What, my dear Lady Disdain! Are you yet living?'"

And then that old theater magic kicked in and I forgot my lines. When I say I forgot them, I don't mean the right words didn't come out of my mouth; they did, all of them, just the way Shakespeare wrote them, just the way I'd rehearsed them in this very spot and just the way I'd spoken them opposite the chalk girl in McGrath's tomb. When I say I forgot my lines, I mean I reached that wonderful moment of onstage levitation that you sometimes feel as an actor if you're very, very lucky: The lines are so much a part of you that you can let them go and forget them; while your body is down there strutting and fretting its hour upon the stage, you can hover like a dust mote in the spotlight and catch a glimpse, just for a second, into what it's all about.

Call it hyperbole, call it whatever you want, but in my split-second moment of levitation I could have sworn I caught a dust-mote glimpse into what would happen next: I would wake brokenhearted at having to leave Morlan, but by midmorning I'd be dizzy with longing for my own room, for River Road, for my CDs and books and for my dad, who would show up in the Munch (the last parent to arrive but still the first person I'd want to see; the tears that would spring to my eyes would surprise and embarrass us both). On the way out of town we'd pass the Egg Drop, and Xiu Li would be waving and Mason would be hunched in a booth, nursing a black coffee before walking the two miles home, where he would discover in his backpack the note I had hidden there, a line borrowed from Yeats: *one (wo!!)man loved the pilgrim soul in you, and loved the sorrows of your changing face . . .*

First, though, he would catch sight of the Munch at the red light and he'd climb up on the table and behind the glass, behind the red-painted words BREAKFAST SERVED ANYTIME, he'd take a deep bow, like he did beneath my window that first day, like he was doing now, and I was bowing with him, hand in hand, and I could see our friends out there beyond the footlights, clapping and smiling and cheering.

I could see that Jessica would follow in her sisters' footsteps to Morlan and she would fall in love with Eric the RA and they would seal their God Match right after graduation; I'd get to be a bridesmaid and the wedding would be gorgeous, something right out of a magazine or a dream, but after that we'd drift the way friends don't mean to do but do. There would be Christmas cards with babies on them. Twins.

Sonya's boyfriend, Kevin Donnelly, would play ball for UK, but in the middle of a game at the newly named arena something strange would happen, his heart would stop; it would turn out to have been enlarged, his heart, or something like that. People would have caught the tragic moment on their phones; a blurry image of Kevin falling to the polished wood floor would make its way to YouTube. It would go viral, and Sonya would go ballistic. She would take her rage and grief to law school and take every bit of law that she could muster into her own hands. She would make huge bank, and she would take her first paycheck to Kevin Donnelly's granny and would be loyal to her (and to me, to Jessica, to the mountains of Eastern Kentucky, to her family and her beautiful black Western Kentucky ancestors, six generations strong) as long as she would continue to breathe.

The seats stretching up behind Sonya and Jessica and the others were almost fully plunged in darkness, but in that dust-mote moment I scanned them still, those back-row seats, for the faces that I would seek in windows and in back rows and in mirrors for always: GoGo's face, smiling at me all the way to graduation and then to NYU and the Tisch School of the Arts, where I would go because the scholarship really would fall out of the sky, just like Carol's dance scholarship to Juilliard would, as if through all those years of dreaming we had willed our magic futures right into place. Alongside the light of GoGo's face would be the darkened shade of my mother's: Eventually I would try to stop imagining her in the windows and back rows of my life, but always she would appear there, because no matter how surely your friends can become your family, no matter how deeply you are cared for by such a lucky windfall of other people's mothers (Carol's, Calvin's, Mason's, each one a gift), the mother you always deep-down want—and you can ask Scout Finch if you don't believe me—is nobody else's but your own.

As for Chloe and Calvin and Mason: They would be true to their words and our Agreement. We'd meet in the fall and everybody's hair would be longer and the leaves would be turning and the plans and applications would be falling into place: Calvin would take the scholarship, would study agriculture and be a first-generation college graduate, would do his family proud and keep the farm, keep it dutifully and lovingly, and keep Holyfield, too, who would live to a ripe old age on fresh air and corn and irreplaceable Kentucky bluegrass and Calvin's singular, honorable brand of love, a love that each one of us would count on (and wonder at, and sometimes take for granted) over the years — and there would be many — to come.

Chloe would surprise us and take the scholarship, too: She'd go straight to the UK study abroad office, first stop Sorbonne, and later, much later, she'd come back to her alma mater and teach French, and one year she'd have this bright-eyed freshman named Juliet Goble-Xavier and the girl would look strangely familiar to Chloe, but the semester would be halfway over and Juliet's French would be perfect before it would click and Chloe would think, *Ah, I knew you when you were a bébé; your father had a hand in changing my life.*

Mason would go to Columbia, but it would be his camera that got him there, not the stage. I'd visit him sometimes in his hovel on Riverside Drive, and sometimes he would come downtown to see Carol and me in our tiny Houston Street apartment, strung with a million tiny white lights. We'd eat steaming noodles from the place downstairs and we would pine for Kentucky stars and sometimes Mason and I would stretch our bodies out—shoulders, hips, fingers barely touching—along the length of the beveled floor, which would rumble at night with the mysterious, subterranean passage of the trains and the great big huge heart of the city, beating its marvelous drum.

A NOTE (& SOME ACKNOWLEDGMENTS) FROM THE AUTHOR:

There's no such place as Morlan College. It's a figment of my imagination, but I feel it's worth mentioning—for anyone who might be interested in this sort of thing—that I borrowed its name from the art gallery at Transylvania University. Transy also has a Kissing Tree (though it's not a sycamore, and there's no swing—the swing can be found on another Kentucky college campus, but I don't want to go revealing all my secrets, do I?), as well as a tomb, secreted away beneath the storied administration building and belonging to one Constantine Rafinesque, who has been haunting the place for almost two hundred years. If when I was applying to colleges the admissions folks at Transy had mentioned the legend of Rafinesque and the annual Halloween lottery that allows a few brave students to spend the night in his tomb, I think I'd have been won over immediately.

Instead, I ended up at the University of Kentucky, where I owe sincere thanks to my unparalleled English and Classics professors who encouraged my writing and gave me an education I wouldn't trade for anything and who in my estimation deserve paychecks equal to or greater than that of the basketball coach—which is not to say I don't love the basketball, because oh, how devotedly I do.

Generous early readers, teacher and librarian colleagues, angels of the Morris Book Shop, the unforgettable Mr. Walsh, who in eleventh grade made us memorize Strunk and White's *Elements of Style* and made all the difference—what if they don't see these acknowledgments? They're busy! There're a thousand laudable reasons they might miss them, and anyway, they deserve so much more. Grateful arms thrown around their necks. Handwritten thank-you notes sent in the mail, brownies made with humility and love. That and more is what's coming to them and to the following, as time and geography allow: Everyone at the Carnegie Center for Literacy and Learning, where all the magic happens. Randi Ewing, this book's fairy godmother from the start. Sarah and Molly and Amy, keepers of all the secrets. The YA Novel Discovery Contest and the She Writes community, who honored this book and set the adventure in motion. The ladies of the Young Women Writers Project, especially Elizabeth Kilcoyne, Annie Griggs, and Annie Bradford. The Kentucky Governor's Scholars Program and Governor's School for the Arts, a golden part of my—and so many other lucky people's—story. Elizabeth Kaplan, agent extraordinaire. Nicole Raymond and her fellow wizards at the magnificent Candlewick Press, where I'm speechlessly honored that this book has found a home. Most of all, my wondrous, irreplaceable family—the cherished one I was born into, the one I was fortunate enough to marry into, the one I find in my friends, and the one I created with Huston Combs (Distinguished Eccentric and modern-day Atticus Finch if ever there was one), who is directly responsible for this book's existence and so much else that is good in my life, especially our wonder boys, who I hope will always treasure books as much as they do right now. I love you all so fiercely, I can just barely stand it. Thank you.